A SEASON
IN THE LIFE OF
EMMANUEL

A SEASON IN THE LIFE OF EMMANUEL

MARIE-CLAIRE BLAIS

Drawings by Mary Meigs

Translated by
DEREK COLTMAN

Introduction by
PRISCILA UPPAL

Essay by
KIRSTY BELL

Exile Editions

*Publishers of singular
Fiction, Poetry, Drama, Non-fiction and Graphic Books*

2008

Library and Archives Canada Cataloguing in Publication

Blais, Marie-Claire, 1939-
[Saison dans la vie d'Emmanuel. English]
    A season in the life of Emmanuel / Marie-Claire Blais ; translated by
Derek Coltman ; illustrations by Mary Meigs ; introduction by Priscila Uppal.

(Exile classics ; 9)

Translation of: Une saison dans la vie d'Emmanuel.

ISBN 978-1-55096-118-8

    I. Coltman, Derek II. Title. III. Title: Saison dans la vie d'Emmanuel.
English. IV. Series.

PS8503.L33S313 2008   C843'.54   C2008-903574-7

All rights reserved
Design and Composition by ReproSet Design
Cover Photograph by Michael Prince/Corbis
Typeset in Garamond and Bembo at the Moons of Jupiter Studios
Printed in Canada by Gauvin Imprimerie

The publisher would like to acknowledge the financial assistance of
The Canada Council for the Arts and the Ontario Arts Council.

 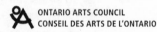

Conseil des Arts   Canada Council   ONTARIO ARTS COUNCIL
du Canada   for the Arts   CONSEIL DES ARTS DE L'ONTARIO

Published in Canada in 2007 by Exile Editions Ltd.
144483 Southgate Road 14
General Delivery
Holstein, Ontario, N0G 2A0
info@exileeditions.com
www.ExileEditions.com

Canadian Sales Distribution: U.S. Sales Distribution:
McArthur & Company   Independent Publishers Group
c/o Harper Collins   814 North Franklin Street
1995 Markham Road   Chicago, IL 60610
Toronto, ON M1B 5M8   www.ipgbook.com
toll free: 1 800 387 0117   toll free: 1 800 888 4741

INTRODUCTION

In his 1966 introduction to the English edition of Marie-Claire Blais' *A Season in the Life of Emmanuel* (first published as *Une Saison dans la Vie d'Emmanuel* in 1965), distinguished American critic Edmund Wilson wrote: "I first read this book in manuscript and wondered whether it could ever be published in Canada." It has since come to be regarded as her masterpiece (it won the Prix France-Canada and the Prix Médicis of France). But Wilson had a point. He saw that her fourth novel signalled a shift away from the unnamed nightmare landscapes of *Mad Shadows*, her first book of "obsessed and tormented dreams," to "the turbid swirling sediment of the actual French-Canadian world."

The distinction here is blurred because Blais' 'actual French-Canadian world' is just as lyrical and intense and phantasmal as the mythical or gothic landscapes of her first works. And once again, Blais never directly identifies Québec, but it is impossible for the reader not to recognize that this is the story of a poor, oversized, mid-twentieth century rural Québecois family with few options open to them (the convent for girls, the Noviciat or shoe factory for boys), a family susceptible to cruelties and brutalities from all sides: the harsh winter landscape, poverty, ignorance, the gothic Catholic Church, sudden increased industrialization, and the treatment of women as sexual vessels and baby-factories. All of this was no doubt shocking to readers of the time, and perhaps still is, for I have heard that there are professors who teach the novel as if it were a parody, as if life in Québec could never have been like that.

But of course it was. That is why in the 1960s, during what is now called The Quiet Revolution, the political and social climate in Québec was in the process of radical readjustment.

Following the death of Provincial Premier Maurice Duplessis and the subsequent dissolution of the decades-long conservative stranglehold on politics in favour of a new liberal government, the largely patriarchal and Church-run province began to secularize. The responsibility for education and health was transferred away from the Catholic Church to the provincial government; more civil rights were granted to women (before 1940 women were not allowed to vote in Québec, and the rights of married women were akin to those of minors and interdicted persons); and the agriculturally based economy began a swift transformation to an industrial and entrepreneurial one. The Québec people, armed with more civil rights and opportunities to guide their own destinies, began to debate the terms of their relationship with the rest of Canada, splitting into the vocal federalist and separatist fractions that remain vitally active today. At the same time, Québec also began to open up to the world – perhaps best exemplified by its hosting of the World's Fair, Expo 67, which was in many ways a coming-out party for Québec, public proof of a growing cosmopolitanism and waning parochialism.

As Québec was changing drastically, the literary landscape also underwent its own revolution. The literature encouraged by the Jansenist Catholic Church in the nineteenth and early-to-mid-twentieth centuries – the morally "sound" tales of Paul Claudel, Louis Hémon, and François Mauriac – gave way to an interest in the previously forbidden André Gide, Albert Camus, and Jean-Paul Sartre, and the cultivation of a passionate and distinctive body of work by radical, subversive, intellectually and aesthetically complex artists who questioned the values and social constructions of the past and interrogated the new ruling systems of their province. Alongside Hubert Aquin, Gérard Bessette, Claude Gavreau, Anne Hébert, Paul-Marie Lapointe, and Gaston Miron, Marie-Claire Blais was one of these literary revolutionaries and arguably she has emerged as the most important. The success in 1965 of *A Season in the Life of Emmanuel* is evidence of her work fulfilling this cultural and aesthetic need.

But this success should not diminish the fact that it was a risky, original offering at the time, and Edmund Wilson was more than justified in his hesitations. The prominent English-Canadian novelist Robertson Davies reviewed it condescendingly in *The New York Times*: "[*A Season in the Life of Emmanuel*] uncomfortably suggests that large group of novels that Stella Gibbons knocked on the head in 1932 with *Cold Comfort Farm*. Nobody in those books was a homosexual, so far as I can recall, and nobody actually got to the point of masturbating or ravishing a hunchback, but the flavor was the same; nature was morose, and man was vile. The revival of this sort of novel in our post-Gibbons era is dangerous even to a talent so strong as that of Mlle. Blais, and we hope she will think better of it when next she publishes." I believe, regardless of our notions of social progress and tolerance, that if such a manuscript – author unknown – were circulated among various Canadian publishing houses now (both Francophone and Anglophone – I would make an even stronger case for the Anglophone publishers) – there's a very good chance it would not see the light of day, certainly not from a big commercial house. Our literary climate at the moment is timid, and timid in the worst way: timid while pretending to be worldly and progressive. *A Season in the Life of Emmanuel* is no parody. Quite frankly, it's too real, and Marie Claire-Blais' descriptions of life are too honest and too brave.

In North America, we live in a culture that welcomes shock, one that invites and exploits horrific and dark representations of contemporary times (we can't seem to exhaust our interest in serial killers, sex offenders, or mobsters, for example). What is distinctive and all-too-rare, however, is the ability to render the dark and tragic boldly on the page while maintaining a sympathetic stance; the ability to articulate, with passion and intelligence, the limitations of the world that desperate characters live in. We prefer black and white morality, and an indulgent, rather than inquisitive, voyeurism. In other words, it's easier to shock an audience than to unsettle it. But unsettling is what true revolution is about. Which is why Marie-Claire Blais' talents are not only distinctive in our times, but vitally necessary.

Marie-Claire Blais achieves a delicate balance of unapologetic naturalism and lyrical expressionism in *A Season in the Life of Emmanuel*. Even the title speaks to these two somewhat contradictory literary modes. The title character has just been "born without fuss, this winter morning" as the novel begins. Grand-mère Antoinette watches over him, and in fact christens him, because his mother is so worn out from taking care of her children and her husband and from the labours of her sixteenth delivery, that she eschews this motherly responsibility. Amid these difficult circumstances, Grand-mère doesn't have much hope for the child's future: "You'll behave just like the others, you'll be ignorant and cruel and bitter . . ."

What follows is a detailed and haunting narrative that switches between multiple stream-of-consciousness perspectives, from baby to Grand-mère to other children in the family – predominantly Jean-Le Maigre, a consumptive with an obsession for writing and reading ("No one can see me when I'm reading," he taunts), who we know after the few first pages will probably not survive the winter; but also Number Seven, Jean-Le Maigre's co-conspirator; and Héloïse, an obsessively pious convent girl who, in her search for the ecstasies of martyrdom, will be ravaged by the passions she has been taught to avoid. The narrative also switches locales from their small cramped homestead, to the rural schoolhouse, the hypocritical convent, and the feared Noviciat. Every scene unfolds in stark, provocative, and sometimes startlingly funny, language with a particular genius for uncovering, without exploiting, each individual's darkest or most tantalizing dreams.

By the time Emmanuel's first season is over, other lives – both physical and emotional – particularly those of his siblings, have been snuffed out. One expects by the title a *bildungsroman*, a coming-of-age novel, one that typically ends with the title character emerging after various trials and tribulations out of childhood to stake his new place in the world. In *A Season in the Life of Emmanuel*, the *bildungsroman* connotations are ironic: the title character is still an infant by the end of the narrative – he has lived through just one season of his life, although by novel's end we understand that this simple feat is a hard-won accomplishment – and some of his older brothers and sisters have indeed entered the wider world and workforce but to almost uniformly disastrous results, while other lives are cut short before reaching adulthood. The seasons persist and the children are like crops. Some make it. Some are harvested and consumed. Some survive despite bad soil and bad tending. Some fail. The cycle continues. And funerals are as much a part of the seasons as are the never-ending births.

Several of the incidents described in the novel are sexually graphic, disturbing, even immoral, and it's hard for me to imagine a writer today describing with such pathos and sensitivity what Marie Claire-Blais has represented here: boys crowded into small beds and masturbating each other at night to keep warm; children drinking themselves into a stupor, anticipating their Friday night beatings; a young woman humiliated by the religious community that she admires, giving herself over to violations of the flesh; a tormented priest hastening the deaths of the weak and sick boys in his care. While the novel certainly invites social critique, the family is never reduced to anything resembling a case study of alcoholism, physical abuse, inadequate social services, or lack of birth control (and in many writers' hands it would be). Blais never exploits the incidents for shock value or to forward a political agenda and she never allows us to vilify a character. She wants us to empathize, to appreciate the complexity, both social and emotional, of each character's situation, the various circumstances and motives that make easy judgments impossible.

What Marie-Claire Blais reveals so persuasively and beautifully is that, even in the midst of sadness, tragedy and hopelessness, the human spirit (when it has the strength) seeks a way out, a reprieve, whether in the small joys of sex and drink, or laughter, music, the imagination. While *A Season in the Life of Emmanuel* accurately describes the fate of a family living in Québec at a particular time in Canadian history, its relevance extends far beyond its historical moment and geographical locale. The fate of this family is the fate of families all over the world who struggle to provide their loved ones with basic necessities: food, shelter, education, solace, happiness. The reason Jean-Le Maigre is such an attractive character and his end the most tragic in the novel – even the "immortal" Grandmère is diminished by his demise – is that through the imagination, and specifically through the reading of books and the act of writing, he manages to transcend his oppressive circumstances, at least for a little while.

Jean-Le Maigre's passionate tenacity in the face of suffering reveals the vital powers of the imagination that are so important to Blais: to rebel, to contradict, to envision new realities, to empathize; in short, to confront limitation with imaginative possibility. When Jean-Le Maigre exclaims, "I'm going to write my posthumous works!" the comment is ironic but, ultimately, genuine. Imagining a future is the first condition of hope. Through his artistic expression, he insists on his right to live and to be remembered. As readers, we are aware that his fate is deeply intertwined with our own.

Marie-Claire Blais has been compared to William Faulkner, Franz Kafka, and Fyodor Dostoyevsky. But comparisons of genius are misleading, for a genius, by definition, is an original. It is a part of her genius that she plunges us into the murky depths of the soul at the same time that she effortlessly lifts us towards transcendence. The best description of her style is found in *A Season in the Life of Emmanuel* itself, in a scene where members of the family are gathered together in mourning at the Noviciat:

> Pomme and Number Seven rubbed their eyes already reddened by emotion. They had never known any music but the quavering hymns sung by the children of Mary in their own parish, or the frail lament from their own church organ, and were filled with wonder by the choir of Novices, whose voices streamed forth untamed from the depths of childhood.

For Emmanuel, childhood has barely begun but, even as a newborn, he is aware that he contains within himself the whole history of his family (as we do ours?) and perhaps even the whole history of Québec, especially a great stubbornness: "The knowledge had come to him that all this misery would never end; but he had consented to live." This great novel continues to have a life, and *should* continue to have a life in the decades, and centuries, to come, because its truths are just as stubborn as its characters, and it is through Marie-Claire Blais' prose, its haunting, melancholic, stubborn beauty that we, too, consent to live.

Priscila Uppal, 2008

Priscila Uppal is an English-Canadian poet, novelist, editor, and professor at York University. Her most recent publications include *Ontological Necessities* (shortlisted for the Griffin Prize for Excellence in Poetry) and the novel *The Divine Economy of Salvation*, published in several languages. Her second novel, *To Whom It May Concern,* and a critical study, *We Are What We Mourn: The Contemporary English-Canadian Elegy,* will be released in early 2009.

I

. . . Grand-mère Antoinette's feet dominated the room. They lay there like two quiet, watchful animals, scarcely twitching at all inside their black boots, always ready to spring into action; two feet bruised by long years of work in the fields (opening his eyes for the first time in the dusty morning light, he couldn't see them yet, was not yet aware of the hidden wound in the leg, beneath the woollen stocking, of the ankles swollen within their prisons of leather and laces . . .), two noble and pious feet (did they not make the journey to church once every morning, even in winter?), two feet brimming with life, and etching forever in the memories of those who saw them, even only once, their sombre image of authority and patience.

Born without fuss, this winter morning, Emmanuel was listening to his grandmother's voice. Immense and all-powerful, she seemed to be ruling the whole world from her armchair. (Don't cry, what have you got to cry about? Your mother has gone back to work on the farm. Just you keep quiet till she gets home. Ah, you're already so selfish, already so wicked. Already in a temper!) He called for his mother. (You've picked a bad time to be born, we've never been so poor, it's a hard winter for everyone, the war, the food shortage, and you the sixteenth too . . .) She sat complaining to herself in a low voice, telling the beads of a grey rosary hanging from her waist. (I've got my rheumatism too, but no one ever mentions it. I have my troubles too. And besides I hate newborn babies; insects they are, crawling around in the dust! You'll behave just like the others, you'll be ignorant and cruel and bitter . . . You didn't give a thought to all the worries you were bringing me, I have to think of everything, what name to give you, the christening . . .)

It was cold inside the house. There were faces all around him; figures kept appearing. He looked at them but didn't recognize them yet. Grand-mère Antoinette was so huge that he couldn't see all of her. He was afraid. He shrank into himself, closing up like a shell. (Enough of that, said the old woman, look around you, open your eyes, I'm here, I give the orders here! Look at me, properly, I am the only one here who is worthy of this house. I am the one who sleeps in the scented room, I store the soap under my bed . . .) "We shall have plenty of time," Grand-mère Antoinette said, "there is no hurry for today . . ."

(His grandmother had a vast bosom, he couldn't see her legs under the heavy skirts, dry sticks, cruel knees, such strange garments swaddling her body as it shivered in the cold.) He tried to hook his delicate fists onto her knees, to bury himself in the cave of her lap (for he was discovering that she was so thin beneath those mountains of cloth, those rough skirts, that for the first time he was not afraid of her). But those woollen clothes still kept him at a distance from the icy bosom, from the breasts she was crushing into herself with one hand in a gesture of alarm or self-defense; for whenever you approached that body, stifled inside its austere dress, you felt that you were approaching some sleeping freshness within her, an ancient and proud desire that none had ever fulfilled – you wanted to go to sleep in her, as in some warm river, to lie and rest upon her heart. But she kept Emmanuel at a distance with that same gesture of the hand that had once rejected love, and punished man's desires.

"Oh Lord, another boy, what is to become of us?" But she quickly regained her confidence: "I am strong, child. You can give your life into my keeping. Put your trust in me."

He listened to her. Her voice rocked him with a monotonous, defeated chant. She wrapped him in her shawl, not fondling him but rather plunging him into the folds of cloth and into the smells of them as though into a bath. He held his breath. Sometimes, without meaning to, she scratched him slightly with her bent fingers; she held him aloft and shook him, and once more he called for his mother. (Bad boy, she said impatiently.) He dreamed of his mother's breast coming to appease his thirst and quiet his rebellious cries.

"Your mother is out working, as usual," Grand-mère Antoinette said. "Today is just a day like any other. You think only of yourself. I've got work to do too. Newborn babies are dirty. They disgust me. But you see, I'm good to you, I wash you, I take care of you, and you will be the first to be glad when I die . . ."

But Grand-mère Antoinette believed herself to be immortal. And her whole triumphant being was immortal for Emmanuel too, as he lay gazing up at her in astonishment. "Ah, my child, no one is listening to you, there is no use in crying. You will soon learn that you're alone in this world! You too will be afraid . . ."

The beams of the sun shone in through the window. In the distance, the landscape was confused, unapproachable. Emmanuel could hear voices, steps all around him. (He trembled with cold as his grandmother washed him, or rather drowned him several times in icy water . . .) "There," she said, "it's all over. There's nothing to be afraid of. I'm here. One gets used to everything, you'll see."

She smiled. He felt the desire to respect her silence; he no longer dared to complain, for it seemed to him suddenly that he had already been familiar for a long while with cold, with hunger, and perhaps even with despair. In the cold sheets, in the cold room, he had suddenly been filled with a strange patience. The knowledge had come to him that all this misery would never end; but he had consented to live. Standing at the window, Grand-mère cried out, almost with joy:

"Here they are. I can feel them coming up the stairs, listen to their voices. Here they all are, the grandchildren, the children, the cousins, the nieces, and the nephews; you think they've been buried under the snow on their way to school, or else dead years ago, but they are always there, under the tables, under the beds, spying on me with their eyes shining in the dark. They are waiting for me to hand out lumps of sugar to them. There are always one or two around my armchair, or my rocking chair when I rock myself of an evening . . .

"They snigger, they play with my shoelaces. They run after me the whole time with that stupid sniggering of theirs, with that begging, hypocritical look in their eyes. I chase them away like flies, but they come back, they fasten themselves on me like a bunch of vermin, they gnaw at me . . ."

Grand-mère Antoinette was admirable as she tamed the tide of children roaring around her feet. (Where did they come from? Did they rise up out of the darkness, out of the black night? They smelled of the night, they spoke with the voice of the night, they crawled around the bed, and they had the familiar smell of poverty . . .)

"Ah, that's enough!" Grand-mère Antoinette said. "I don't want to hear another sound from any of you, out of my way all of you, go back to your beds . . . Vanish, I don't want to see any more of you, ah! heavens, what a smell!"

But then, accompanying the distribution with a few blows of her cane, she handed out the lumps of sugar they were waiting for with open mouths, panting with impatience and hunger, the sugar, the crumbs of chocolate, all the grimy treasures she had accumulated and now emptied out again from her skirts and from her strait-laced bodice. "Get away, get away," she cried.

She drove them off with an all-powerful hand (later, he was to see her walking in the same way through a host of chickens, and rabbits, and cows, sowing curses broadcast as she went, to recover some tearful baby that had fallen in the mud), she beat them back toward the staircase, still throwing them the lumps of sugar, which they scrabbled for, this flood of children, of animals, that later, once again, would emerge from their mysterious lair and come back, scratching at the door anew, to beg from their grandmother.

His mother came in. He recognized her. She didn't come over to him, not at first. He was ready to believe she had deserted him. He recognized her sad face, her drooping shoulders. She didn't seem to remember having brought him into the world that very morning. She was cold. He saw her hands clenching around the brimming milk pail. (He's over there, Grand-mère Antoinette said, he's hungry, he's been crying all day.) His mother was silent. She would always be silent. Some of his brothers were coming back from school and knocking the snow off their boots against the door. (Come here, Grand-mère said, but she hit out at them lightly with the tip of her cane when they passed under the lamp.) In the distance the sun was still red on the hill.

"And Number Seven, what have you done with Number Seven? As long as I live, you'll continue to go to school . . ."

His mother's waist was gently bellying out: she was bending over as she set down the second pail of milk.

"To think they've gone and lost Number Seven in the snow again," Grand-mère Antoinette said.

The bucket ran over. Little drops of milk rolled across the floor in the lamplight. Grand-mère was scolding, reprimanding, sometimes slapping a chapped cheek as it passed within her reach.

"You ought to thank me, ah! if I weren't here you'd never get to school, would you, eh?"

"Grand-mère," a man's voice said from the depths of the kitchen, "school isn't necessary."

The man's voice was merely a murmur. It faded, it disappeared. Standing leaning against the wall, her head tilted slightly onto one shoulder, his mother listened in silence. Perhaps she was asleep. Her dress was open, showing her pale, drooping breasts. Her sons looked at her in silence, and they too were waiting, waiting for night to fall on the hill.

"A hard winter," the man said, rubbing his hands together over the stove. "But perhaps it will be a good spring . . ."

He removed his snow-soaked clothes. He put them to dry on a chair near the fire. He took off his thick boots, then his socks. The smell of wet clothing spread through the house.

(He had taken everything from his mother's heart, he had drunk all her milk with an avid mouth, and now he pretended to be asleep . . .)

"There are orphanages too," the man's voice said.

"I prefer the Noviciat," Grand-mère Antoinette replied. "It doesn't cost anything, and they teach them how to behave."

"But I don't understand what they need all this schooling for," the father muttered into his beard.

"Ah! Men don't understand about these things," Grand-mère Antoinette said with a sigh. "But Grand-mère," the man's voice continued in the depths of the kitchen, while the flames flickered slowly up from the stove (and a little girl at the window looked out with boredom at the setting sun, hands clasped behind her back), "Grand-mère, I know more about life than you do, I know what my children are destined for!"

"For God!" Grand-mère Antoinette replied.

His mother took him in her arms. She was protecting him now with her fragile body, supporting his head so that he could feed and drink in peace; but Grand-mère's long silhouette was still keeping watch, very close, driven by some strange duty to find out what was happening in the hidden parts of his being, sometimes interrupting the insipid meal he was absorbing in a dream. (He was draining his mother, he was drinking up everything inside her!) She, his mother, said nothing, no longer answering, calm, deep, deserted perhaps. He was there, but she had forgotten him. He was producing no echo in her, either of joy or of desire. He slipped into her and lay there without hope.

"That child sees everything," Grand-mère Antoinette said, "you can't hide anything from him." (What shall we call him? David? Joseph? There have been too many Josephs in recent generations. They were weak men! The Emmanuels have all been strong, they took good care of their land.)

"Let us call him Emmanuel."

His mother listened solemnly. Sometimes she lifted her head in surprise, her lip trembled, and she seemed to want to say something, but she said nothing. They heard her sigh, then go to sleep.

"We must settle when he is to be baptized," Grand-mère said.

The father spoke of waiting until spring. "Spring is a good time for baptisms," he said.

"Next Sunday," Grand-mère Antoinette said. "And I'll take him down to be baptized myself."

The mother bowed her head.

"My wife thinks Sunday will do very well too," the man said.

She sat there in her armchair, majestic and contented, and the dark spread little by little over the hill, veiling the white forest and the silent fields. (You should thank me for taking these decisions out of your hands, Grand-mère Antoinette thought in her armchair.)

The man yawned beside the fire. Grand-mère Antoinette was throwing him fleeting, sidelong glances. No, I shall not lift a finger to serve that man, she thought to herself. He thinks I shall do as my daughter does; but I won't bring him his bowl of warm water, or his clean clothes. No, no, I won't budge from my armchair. He is expecting a woman to come and wait on him. But I won't get up.

But something moved beneath the pointed toe of her boot, something shapeless that she tried to push away. Lord! a mouse, a squirrel, there's something under my dress . . .

"Go back to the school and bring back Number Seven, I'll teach him to dawdle about on the roads. Put on your boots, go on, you. You're not to go out, Jean Le Maigre, you're coughing too much! Where were you just then? Were you reading under the table again?"

"I'll burn your book for you," the father's voice said. "I've told you, Grand-mère, we don't want books in this house."

"Jean Le Maigre is talented; Monsieur le Curé said so," Grand-mère Antoinette replied.

"He's consumptive," the man said, "what good can it possibly do him to learn anything? I can't think what that Curé thinks he's about – there's nothing to be done with Jean Le Maigre. He's got one lung rotting away!"

His mother listened. Tomorrow, at the same hour, they would say the same words all over again, and she would make that same slight movement of the head, that sign of silent protest in Jean Le Maigre's defence, but, like today, she would merely listen, say nothing, perhaps feel astonishment that life should repeat itself with such precision, and she would think again: "How long the night's going to be." A strand of hair fell across her brow; she had already closed her eyes, and now she bent over her latest child, her face still gloomy and half asleep.

Standing on one leg, book in hand, Jean Le Maigre gazed searchingly at the newborn infant with a moist gaze. "Who's he?" he asked, without interest. Without waiting for the reply, he coughed, sneezed, and disappeared again behind his book.

"I can see you, Jean Le Maigre," Grand-mère said. "You think you're safe, but I can see you."

"You can't see me. No one can see me when I'm reading," Jean Le Maigre answered.

"Watch out then; I'm going to make you drink your syrup soon," Grand-mère said.

"I'm not here," Jean Le Maigre replied. "I'm dead."

"Perhaps you are," was Grand-mère's reply, "but I'm alive, and as long as I'm alive you'll drink your syrup."

"But what good can it possibly do?" the man's voice asked. The old woman thought of pronouncing one of the curses that the man beside the stove was calmly expecting; he was shrugging his shoulders, already feeling the pleasurable blow of her insult. But Grand-mère Antoinette, disdainfully smiling in her armchair, chose to remain silent – no, this time she would not say that word, she would remain proud and unapproachable. "Well," the man said, turning toward the stove, with its now dying fire, "you're right, Grand-mère, it's just as well they should get used to going to school in winter . . ."

Grand-mère Antoinette, speaking in a clipped, contemptuous tone, replied that she had known harder winters than any of them, and the man, dressing himself clumsily in the shadows, suddenly felt the familiar, daily sense of shame that only the presence of this woman could inspire in him. "Winters as black as death," Grand-mère Antoinette went on, with contempt for the man's body, watching him out of the corner of one eye. "Oh! It's not the first I've seen . . ."

"Yes, it's a gloomy evening," the man commented in weary tones. With his dirt-blackened nails, Jean Le Maigre was gracefully turning the pages of his book. As happy as a prince in his tattered clothes, he was in a hurry to read it.

"Oh heavens, how funny it is," he exclaimed through a wild burst of laughter.

"I wouldn't laugh if I were you," the father said. "I might take that book of yours away from you."

Jean Le Maigre shook his head, revealing the pale brow beneath his hair. "It's too late, I've read every page. You can't burn the pages I've read. They're all written here!"

For the first time, the man raised his eyes in a sombre gaze toward the mother and child. Then he forgot them again immediately. He looked at the bowl of dirty water on the stove. He was beginning to feel more and more constricted in his waistcoat.

"It's stifling in here," he said.

The button suddenly burst off his shirt collar. "It's not going to be me who sews that button on," Grand-mère Antoinette said. "You know it'll be you," the man replied, "it is always you, Grand-mère!"

"Jean Le Maigre," Grand-mère said, raising a triumphant head to look at her grandson, "listen, the Noviciat . . . There are infirmaries, warm dormitories . . . You'd like it there . . ."

"Oh, Grand-mère," Jean Le Maigre replied from behind his book, "let me read in peace and cough in peace, since I enjoy it."

Jean Le Maigre coughed again. Oh Lord, it felt so good! He sneezed, he laughed, he wiped his nose on his dirty shirt.

"Grand-mère," he said, "I know this book by heart now."

"I'm going to give him a hiding, that Jean Le Maigre of yours," the father's voice said.

"Come over by me," Grand-mère Antoinette said to Jean Le Maigre. "No one can hurt you when you're near me."

Jean Le Maigre scratched his nose, then his ears. "What is it now," Grand-mère Antoinette asked. "Nothing," Jean Le Maigre replied. She pulled the ragged child against her, brushed the thin fringe of hair back from his forehead, and made a discovery that astounded no one.

"My God, his head is full of lice again!"

II

Then, tottering with fever but still laughing, Jean Le Maigre offered his head up to the torture. Like a conqueror, Grand-mère Antoinette drew the lamp toward her, then the bowl, and counted the lice as they fell under her cruel comb. His sisters (the little A's, Helena, Maria), with wild, shy eyes and sulky lips, approached on tiptoe. They huddled against one another or hung back against the wall as they waited for their turn. They fiddled with the ends of their braids. "It's too crowded," Grand-mère Antoinette said. "I don't want to see all these children around me like this! No, oh heavens no!"

And the moment she began to push Jean Le Maigre away from her, his proud head was already raised, he had already escaped from his grandmother's hands with the agility of a fox, just as Number Seven, whom they no longer expected to see, whom they had thought buried beneath the snow or devoured by wolves – Number Seven, with his orange hair, somersaulted over the doorstep, kicked in by his gang of brothers. Grand-mère abandoned her task, broke through the line of little girls: *"What has he been doing this time?* ah! I know all! The little monster, he reeks of alcohol!"

His mother sometimes made a shadowy gesture, an imperceptible sign of surrender or agonized pity, when, escaping from the blows of his elder brothers, Number Seven threw himself on his knees in front of his father. "No forgiveness this evening," Grand-mère Antoinette said.

(Jean Le Maigre and the little girls were giggling in the shadows away from the lamp.) "No, it's all over, I won't let you forgive him again . . ."

Number Seven pretended he found it funny too. (What he most feared was when his father unbuckled his belt and his grandmother cried out as each blow fell: "There, there, on your behind, my boy!")

Afterward he felt better. It was warmer now, and there was a delicious flame flicking up his throat. "This time I was beaten till I bled," Number Seven thought as he stood up again, but he also seemed to be saying to them all: "Thank you very much, I had a marvellous time." He put his hat and his worn-through mittens back on again. "Get undressed," Grand-mère Antoinette said.

"Next time I shall throw you back out again. Not today, there's a storm coming up. Tomorrow!"

The snow was melting on Number Seven's boots. It was running off his stiffened clothes and hair. Jean Le Maigre, already long accustomed to his brother's caprices, wiped up the trickles of water behind him and brushed off the snow still clinging to his coat.

"I don't like seeing them together," Grand-mère Antoinette said. "No, I don't like seeing devils plotting together at all!"

"Ah," Number Seven said, staggering with drunkenness against Jean Le Maigre's shoulder, "ah, you just don't know how warm it makes you! How good it makes you feel . . ."

"Take off your hat," Jean Le Maigre answered. "You heard, take off your hat. Tell me, is it burning a bit?"

"It's all right for you. You're lucky, being so thin. Who's going to beat you like that, eh?"

"No one," Jean Le Maigre replied, lying as usual and thinking with pride of the burning weals across his body, of all the blows borne in silence, head high and heart light.

"At your age I always got to school first, you know! I really am ashamed for you," said Jean Le Maigre with a shrug of his shoulders.

"Liars, hoodlums," Grand-mère Antoinette called out as she saw the pair of them staggering and laughing past her, their arms around each other's necks.

"Your father is right, Jean Le Maigre, you're rotten to the core!"

And the old woman, picking a blond braid at random, tugged one of the little girls over her knees, where the child bent, sobbing, not knowing why this rasping and violent hand, only too skilled at hunting lice, had fallen upon her timid head . . .

At that late evening hour, Jean Le Maigre and Number Seven, careless of their grandmother's scolding cries, were in the cellar, singing and drinking as they smoked the butts that Number Seven collected after school, during his idle wanderings along the road.

"Drinking with me is one thing, but drinking without me is not allowed. Do you understand?"

Number Seven signalled his assent with a wink. His face was so white in the flickering candlelight that Jean Le Maigre thought he must be sick.

"Give me that candle," Jean Le Maigre said severely.

Sitting on an enormous crate of potatoes, Number Seven was playing at making the holes in his socks bigger.

"I feel good, hic . . . It's hot, but I feel good, hic! I could even write a poem now, just like that, without a moment stopping . . . Hic! Hic!"

"You've got the hiccups! For God's sake, do you want them to hear us in the loft?"

"Hic . . . hic . . . they'll go away soon, hic . . . hic . . ."

"At least I know how to drink, it doesn't make me sick."

But his hand shook slightly as it held the candle. "How strange the moon is this evening in the sky!" Jean Le Maigre sighed, gazing at the slender beams of light striking the brick floor. "Heavens, I've never seen it look like this!"

"But there isn't a moon tonight," Number Seven replied, turning incredulously toward Jean Le Maigre, his little face ravaged with fatigue. "Where can you see a moon, eh?"

"You drink too much," Jean Le Maigre said (pouring himself another glass, ignoring his brother's). "At your age I was doing something useful, learning Latin, having brilliant conversations with Monsieur le Curé. But you . . ."

Number Seven was dozing against his shoulder . . . "Hic . . . hic . . ." he murmured, like a baby complaining in its sleep, nestling his face beneath Jean Le Maigre's pointed chin. "Hic . . . I feel really good!"

Abandoning his brother to his drunken sleep, Jean Le Maigre opened his book, its pages yellowed by the damp. The book was full of fabulous meals, and as the scent of new bread suddenly wafted out from its pages, Jean Le Maigre felt a slight pang in his empty stomach. *"The girl,"* Jean Le Maigre read silently, *"the girl brought in the fresh bread and the steaming soup, the girl . . ."*

Jean Le Maigre was hungry, there was no further doubt.

"I'm going to look for something to eat in the kitchen," he said, shaking his sleeping brother by the arm. "I'm not afraid of my father, not me. I never ask his pardon. I slip under the table, between their legs, and zip . . . I steal a piece of meat, a slice of bread. And that's it. Then we can eat it together in peace."

"If I were you," Number Seven said, "I'd ask his pardon. Yes, before I stole the meat."

But Jean Le Maigre was no longer there.

There was not much to eat, but the father and the elder sons had brutish appetites that filled Grand-mère Antoinette with indignation as she sat there at the end of the table, looking down from a chair that was too high for her. Perched there like a crow, she gave a little curt "Ah" of disapproval every time some froth-coated sliver of food fell from her son-in-law's greedy lips. The men and the boys sat as if in a trance around the table, protecting their plates like so many hoards of treasure, and they ate without raising their eyes. Taking advantage of their miserly silence, Jean Le Maigre slid under the table on all fours, and sitting there surrounded by the heavy, apparently lifeless legs sloping toward him, he imagined himself lost in the middle of a field of rank-smelling feet, watching the strange movements of those naked extremities beneath the table. Between his father's legs, as though through the dark banisters of a staircase, he could see his mother coming and going in the kitchen with plates of food. She always looked exhausted and dead-eyed. Her face was the colour of the earth. He watched her preparing the thick, greasy food that the men devoured, with customary greed, as fast as she could bring it in. He felt sorry for her. He felt sorry too for those heavy children she carried absent-mindedly around with her every year, dark burdens against her heart. But sometimes he forgot his mother's presence completely and thought only of the companion imprisoned in the cellar, with whom he would later share his evening meal. Grand-mère Antoinette was an accomplice in these thoughts. Salt, cheese, small pieces of food snatched up here and there with a fearless hand, all vanished beneath the table. But meat, no! "If you think," she said to herself, "if you think I'm going to give you meat for Number Seven – no, I'll never consent to that!"

Jean Le Maigre tickled his grandmother's ankle under the table. "Ah, if he could only live till spring," Grand-mère Antoinette thought. "December, January, February, if he could only live till March, oh Lord, if he could only live till summer comes . . . Funerals are such a nuisance for everyone!" But this computation of the months that were still separating her from Jean Le Maigre's tragic death did not prevent her grandson from behaving as usual like a little devil! Though he was making painful efforts not to betray his presence: fighting down the sharp cough rising in his throat. He was afraid of awakening his father's slumbering wrath. His grandmother was meanwhile imagining the good meal that would follow his funeral. (A consoling image of death, for Monsieur le Curé was so generous toward families in mourning; she could see him already, eating and drinking on her right; and on her left, as though in heaven already, Jean Le Maigre, clean, his hair neatly combed, and dressed in clothes as white as snow.) There had been so many funerals during the years that Grand-mère Antoinette had reigned in her house, so many little black corpses, in the wintertime, children always disappearing, babies who had lived only a few months, adolescents who had vanished mysteriously in the fall, or in the spring. Grand-mère Antoinette allowed herself to be rocked gently in the swell of all those deaths, suddenly submerged in a great and singular feeling of content.

"Grandma," Jean Le Maigre begged under the table, "just one piece, just a crumb . . ."

Grand-mère raised the corner of the tablecloth and saw a great, black eye shining in the darkness. So you're there, are you, she thought, disappointed at finding him still alive as usual, with one hand stretched out toward her, like a dog's paw. But when all was said and done, she'd rather have him like this; yes, it was better than the splendour of a scrubbed and sparkling angel sitting at that macabre banquet – it was better, this vision of an ordinary Jean Le Maigre in his rags beneath the table, raising a timid forehead as he begged from her.

"How well I've eaten," said Jean Le Maigre, astonished to be lying once again, and above all to be lying with such joy! Suddenly he saw only one remedy for all these lies that flowed from his lips in such an inexhaustible flood: confession, a real confession on his knees in front of the stinking confessional (but Jean Le Maigre was not aware of unpleasant smells, thanks to his blocked-up nose, and only sensed the rare perfumes that sometimes came within his ken), and so he saw himself, murmuring his sins into the indiscreet ear of a priest, taking pleasure in his self-betrayal, stirring up his basest secrets in a fantasy of delight!

"Well," Number Seven asked, lying in pale collapse among the brown potatoes, "can you still see the moon?"

"I was just thinking that you've drunk too much," Jean Le Maigre answered. "You ought to make your confession, yes, right away, without thinking about it . . . A real confession, a general confession! In other words, you must tell me about all the wicked things you've ever done, and there are lots of them, as I know only too well! You must tell me everything, and then I'll give you absolution. Afterward you can start all over again, if you want."

After this speech, Jean Le Maigre, bending his head and imitating the Curé's voice, said solemnly: "Speak, my child, I am listening."

"Evening prayers!" Grand-mère Antoinette cried. "Everyone into the living room!"

But as soon as they left the meal table the elder brothers had vanished behind the smoke from their pipes, followed by their father, who was yawning with fatigue, the fly of his trousers flapping in front of him. (Grand-mère Antoinette would pull them, one by one, from behind the shelter of their beards and their newspapers; and they would kneel down with her on the cold floor.)

If they weren't in the cellar, Jean Le Maigre and Number Seven would escape through the kitchen and out into the snowy night as soon as it was time for prayers. All tangled up in their bootlaces, coats hurriedly thrown over their shoulders, the little girls too ran eagerly out to the latrines. Jean Le Maigre and Number Seven stood and made fun of them as they came back, coughing into their hair. The two boys smoked while they waited standing under the trees, or sometimes, when they couldn't push their way past the file of little girls tripping and shoving their way into the backhouse, they urinated into the snow, without interrupting their peaceful conversation. Once shut in the latrines, they sat and read the whole of the Curé's library, or wrote high-flown verses such as Jean Le Maigre's poem that began and ended with the lines:

> *How funereal the snow*
> *Beneath the black flight of the birds . . .*

Whereas Number Seven, alas, could often find nothing in his head but lines like "My heart is full of garbage" and "I'm cold, I'm losing my teeth and my hair . . ."

At eight o'clock, Grand-mère Antoinette came out to retrieve with imperious hand any deserter, girl or boy, still dreaming on the wooden seat, in the night-filled privy.

Jean Le Maigre stood up. "That's enough," he said. "I don't want to hear any more. As heaven is my witness, I don't wish to hear more!"

"I only did it once," Number Seven said, by way of excuse.

"And now he is lying too! He has dared to lie!"

Then he leaded toward Number Seven and in a low voice asked: "But what was it like, exactly?"

Number Seven lowered his eyes. "The candle's almost out," he said gloomily.

"I see," Jean Le Maigre said. "In other words, you feel no remorse."

"I do feel remorse," Number Seven answered in a timid voice, "but it was very nice at the time."

"Ah!" That's it, that's what vice is like," Jean Le Maigre exclaimed, "I understand. But tell me everything. I have to know. First of all, there you were, outside, in the snow. Is that it?"

"Heavens, no. You've got the wrong story," Number Seven replied. "It was in May, and it was hot, in the schoolyard. There were flowers, and raspberries too."

"There aren't any raspberries in May," Jean Le Maigre said sententiously.

"It must have been later on then," said Number Seven, who, despite his tender years, had already wandered idly through a good many summers and winters (seasons that Jean Le Maigre liked to keep separate in his recollections – remembering how it had been a burning summer along the road, still retaining a deep memory of his hunger and his fatigue – or a harsh winter, spent running through the woods. Jean Le Maigre loved to recall all these vanished moments endlessly . . .).

"For heaven's sake, tell! Tell what it was like!"

Number Seven told about the little hunchback girl they had undressed together, in the schoolyard, one day in spring.

"It's your sin, not mine!" Jean Le Maigre protested. (All the same, there were raspberries, Number Seven insisted, and the bees were buzzing . . .)

"What a nice little hunchback she was!" Jean Le Maigre sighed. "Next day she gave me some pancakes. Another day she brought me some paper and pencils. I wrote some poems." (He did not add that his grandmother threw them into the fire that same night, exclaiming that they were scandalous, that Jean Le Maigre would go to hell, so shocked by the title, *To the Warm Beloved*, that she had been afraid to read any further.)

"She was nice," Jean Le Maigre said, "she always went to Mass. She had a beautiful missal with gilt edges."

"And now?" Number Seven asked.

"Ah, now! Now she's a real young lady, she lives in town, she still makes pancakes. But she's aged a great deal," Jean Le Maigre said in a tone of respect. "I suppose all little hunchback girls age quickly. And they're the ones I like best."

He stopped speaking to spit on the floor before Number Seven's admiring gaze.

III

"Héloïse," Grand-mère Antoinette cried, shaking from her bosom the cluster of grandchildren who had been lulled there by the long monotonous prayer, closing their eyes, sucking their thumbs, and dozing off to sleep. "Come down, Héloïse!" And down she came, calm and suffering, her gaze lost in some strange dream. She was still wearing the stiff uniform of the convent she had left a few months before. Homesick for those protective walls, for the mute companions with whom she had shared a heroic patience that she supposed was virtue, Héloïse was thinking that of all those happy days she had preserved nothing but the heavy crucifix now hanging on the wall of her rat-infested room. The crucifix no longer inspired her with anything but terror – and with that terror there came, too, the passion for sacrifice that filled her with ecstasy when she was fasting. But what is a fast in a lonely bedroom, far from the convent? Oh, how impoverished the martyrdom that is suffered without ardour! Héloïse was bored. Every day, Grand-mère would go up and set a frugal meal wrapped in a page of the Saturday paper outside the young girl's bedroom door. (Who knows, Grand-mère thought, perhaps she is a saint?) But soon, angered by Héloïse's stubborn refusal to eat, her grandmother began going up to her door less often and contented herself with shouting up the stairs: "Come down, Héloïse! It's time for prayers!"

Grand-mère Antoinette still said, "We have a saint in the house," when she met Monsieur le Curé. But since the Curé himself ate well and only fasted on Good Fridays (and even then he would break his fast to drink a glass of beer), Grand-mère Antoinette, in her heart of hearts, had by now consigned the young girl's extravagant piety to oblivion. Though Jean Le Maigre and Number Seven, while being soundly thrashed by their father, would still hear the words: "And your sister, your poor sister who's been fasting for a week now . . ." – which never failed to bring grimaces of disgust to their indignant faces.

"You're telling me," Jean Le Maigre would say. "They won't even let you go to hell your own way these days. Honestly, I'm ashamed to see her fasting away like that! It's just egotism, it's not for you and me she's starving herself to death, it's just to make trouble for us. Oh, these virtuous people, they make me sick!"

"But you and me, we can't understand such things . . ." So Number Seven would answer, for he was attracted in some vague way to the mystery surrounding Héloïse. "It's not her fault if she was born religious!"

As Jean Le Maigre had written in one of his numerous chapters devoted to a *Portrait of Héloïse*: "Héloïse displayed this love of suffering even as a child. When everyone around her was milking cows, Héloïse would be meditating, kneeling in the hay, her arms spread out to form a cross, or else watching the drops of blood welling from her fingers where she had pricked them with pins. How many times my grandmother must have wrested from her hands the sword and the crown of thorns with which she religiously punished herself on Fridays."

"That's enough," Grand-mère Antoinette would say, for she never went beyond the bounds of moderation herself. (Or, if she did go beyond them, then it was only through pride, or so she believed.) "Calm down a little."

A stranger to work, contemptuous of her sisters, all of whom were transformed at about the age of thirteen into heavy-bodied young women who toiled in the fields like sturdy young men, disdainful of their swollen faces, their thickened ankles, their reddened hands – Héloïse, with the help of her grandmother, who wanted to get this girl and her precocious vocation settled as quickly as possible and had attempted to shut away her whole family in the Noviciat at one time or another – Héloïse chose the convent.

"You'll be able to find a bit of peace for yourself there," Grand-mère Antoinette told her. "God doesn't like fanatics like you all that much!"

Although still very young, Héloïse was already dried up like a dead twig. "If I were you, I'd try and bloom a bit," Grand-mère Antoinette said as she took her leave. "Eat, it'll do you good." And Héloïse, discovering with surprise that the convent rule was mild, gave herself up to it like one discovering the joys of love for the first time. She emerged from her ecstasies with all her senses renewed, with a strange awareness of life. The nights seemed cooler, and the dawn, scarcely muted at all by the bars on her window, intensely beautiful. All these emotions drained her energies, and she no longer had the strength to pray. Her meditations were drowned in a flood of pagan reflections. Though she used up every ounce of courage she possessed in not rushing to the refectory ten times a day, she still could not prevent herself from suffering the temptation of gluttony when the bell sounded at noon. The delicate food, the carefully prepared dishes, the whiteness of her sheets, and, without her knowing it, the voices of the other nuns, all contributed to the awakening of a fine and menacing sensuality. Héloïse's temptations were directed not only toward food, but more and more toward something else, something which she herself did not recognize as desire because it never took any precise form in her imagination, but which was in fact nothing but aimless desire in search of a goal.

For some time, clothed in clever disguises, this desire wandered from one face to another, from her cell companion to the young man who came with the eggs every morning. It slid into Héloïse's heart without leaving a trace of its passage, brought into being by a single tender word, by the sparkling laughter of a young novice, by a maternal gesture from the Mother Superior; and Héloïse gave in to it without knowing. Little by little, she lost the serenity she had enjoyed for so short a time, and yielding to her scruples, she fell back into prayer as though into a trap. Her excessive piety and the brutal privations she imposed on herself attracted the attention of the Mother Superior, who did not like the established order of her convent disturbed by individual ecstasies. And since she had no patience with sicknesses of the soul she quickly interrupted Héloïse's confidences with a brusque: "You must take a purge, my daughter. That will make you feel better!" Héloïse wiped away a few tears and decided to change her confessor. The new confessor was a young man scarcely out of the Seminary, pimply-faced, his head shaven. No sooner had his sad gaze, full of wild compassion for a distress of a soul only too like his own, fallen upon Héloïse, than she felt herself falling in love with him. Several months later, Héloïse returned home with a letter from the Mother Superior. The letter spoke of nervous exhaustion and attacks of hysteria; Grand-mère Antoinette said that nuns' handwriting was always illegible, and destroyed the letter. Héloïse went up to her room and did not come down again to eat that evening, or any other evening.

Héloïse had closed her eyes. She was praying a little to one side, far from her brothers and the younger children. The *Aves*, full of melancholy, streamed from her lips like a lament. The only response to them came from a few of the hardiest girls – the ones Jean Le Maigre referred to as the big A's – Aurelia Anita Anna . . . The men's voices had fallen silent, and Grand-mère, surrounded by her huddle of little children, only opened her mouth to say *A-men, A-men*. Héloïse spoke in a voice made weak by fasting: at times she murmured, *My God, my God*, as though she were about to suffocate, and her grandmother, in the distance, answered *A-men, A-men*! And suddenly there was a moment of silence.

In the cellar, Jean Le Maigre and Number Seven had suspended their confession to tell each other's fortune with the cards. "Your future is dark," said Number Seven, "very dark, it goes out like a candle. If I were you, I'd ask to have the last rites administered right away. Then it would be over and done with. And then you never know, it might cure you."

"Oh," rejoined Jean Le Maigre, "if you think I'm going off up to heaven like a good boy just like that, with a blessing, then you're wrong!" (He sniffed deeply.) "I have an idea," he said. "I'm going to write my posthumous works!"

"I once knew a man who was very ill," said Number Seven (he did not dare admit that he had greatly enjoyed Grand-père Napoléon's death agony), "iller than you are, he used to cough and spit blood." ("But I spit blood too," Jean Le Maigre put in, offended that any-one should show a lack of respect toward an illness he loved like a sister.) "He was given the Last Sacrament, and the next day he was better. He went out and chopped wood, just as he'd always done."

"But I don't want to get up again and go out chopping wood once I'm dead," Jean Le Maigre said. "I shall put on my wings and I shall fly away." ("But where to?" Number Seven asked uneasily . . .) "You'll stay behind here, you'll have to get up at six in the morning and go out to chop wood. I shall fly about in the sky like a dove."

"A dove?" Number Seven asked doubtfully.

"Why not a dove?" Jean Le Maigre replied, slipping the card out of sight in his pocket.

Number Seven shuffled the cards. "Beware of a woman," he said. "She wants to take you with her into the town. She has evil intentions." "Oh Lord," Jean Le Maigre said in a panic, "that's Grand-mère Antoinette and her Noviciat again!" "But there's someone who wishes you well. He's a very kind person." ("Let me see," Jean Le Maigre said.) "He's good and well behaved, but no one understands him," Number Seven went on. "Good and well behaved inside, but he's also a thief. No one's a bigger thief than he is. He doesn't want you to go into the town, but because he's brave he won't shed a single tear when you go."

"Heavens, that's you!" Jean Le Maigre broke in. "The thief is you!"

"Me, a thief?" Number Seven rejoined. "I'm nothing of the kind."

"Thefts, thefts upon thefts," Jean Le Maigre said. "I can see them swimming before my eyes, like microbes in a pond. Three oranges, a bicycle wheel, a skate, a pair of scissors. And lower down, I see worse crimes. Too many crimes. You have gone too far; there will be no absolution this evening. A chicken? Yes, a chicken. And a fox. That was a double crime, because you sold the skin. A whole family of cats thrown down a well. They will pursue you till the end of your days. Terrible torments await you, my child (you will be tormented like a monk tormented by the devil!)."

"Oh heavens," Number Seven said, "can you see the hares too? All the hares with the little splashes of blood on their tails?"

"They are gliding across the snow. They are there," Jean Le Maigre replied. "They are wagging their ears. They are waiting for you to restore them to life. There are too many crimes on your conscience; you ought to take a bath this evening (since there is no tub, that would be difficult), but it would be better if you didn't go to bed with all those crimes on your conscience. Your feet are dirty," Jean Le Maigre continued, "it would be better if you didn't sleep with me tonight. And your hands are stained with blood. I don't want to sleep with a murderer.

"But you have a generous soul," he went on, "you have already accepted your punishment." (Jean Le Maigre and Number Seven had both spent a part of their youth in Reform School.) "It is very possible that they may hang you one day. Don't forget me at the hour of your death, when the magpies are eating your nose!"

"The candle is going out," said Number Seven. "And I can hear footsteps. We'd better go upstairs right away."

"Don't forget me," Jean Le Maigre answered, "for I too have crimes on my conscience. My soul is no longer at peace, I don't sleep any more, I grind my teeth." (Jean Le Maigre was taking wing, Number Seven was afraid his grandmother was about to appear. "Oh God," he thought, "he's going to start reciting poems again . . .")

> *My head is an aquarium full of floating things,*
> *Your crimes and my crimes*
> *Like sea horses swimming . . .*

"Oh, how horrible it all is," said Number Seven, and then, in an attempt to impress his brother, went on:

> *In my soup as I eat*
> *I see them as they swim, the fish,*

The cats and the foxes,
As I remember the murders I have done,
I lose my appetite . . .

Grand-mère Antoinette put a stop to Number Seven's deplorable lyric strains with a shout of "Héla! What's this I see in my potatoes?" which caused Jean Le Maigre and Number Seven to shift their ground rapidly into the laundry basket, the former burying himself beneath a mass of petticoats, the latter left with his red hair protruding from a flurry of sheets. Number Seven was the first to emerge. Jean Le Maigre, benefiting from his grandmother's clement mood, remained at the bottom of the basket. "I'm not even going to bother to speak to you," Grand-mère Antoinette said. "It's not worth wasting a single word on a good-for-nothing

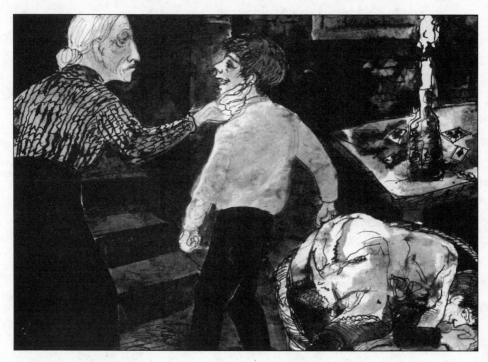

like you." And gripping Number Seven's ear, she pushed him toward the staircase.

Number Seven went on imploring his grandmother for forgiveness, but she curtly rejected his pleas. "You should think yourself lucky it wasn't your father," she said. "If I'd let him come down to the cellar, your bottom would be so red by now you'd never be able to sit on a school bench again." Number Seven didn't like the image much, but the idea of never again sitting on a school bench brought him some comfort.

"You should think yourself lucky," Grand-mère Antoinette repeated, holding Number Seven's head under the water with one hand and working the pump handle with the other.

"Cold water can do you nothing but good!"

The little girls were laughing and clapping their hands.

"Anita, Roberta!" Grand-mère Antoinette cried. "Get these little devils into bed for me!"

Roberta Anna Anita moved forward like a slow herd of cows, each encircling in her thick arms a lively little girl with braided hair, who in a few years would look just like them, and like them also, under the yoke of fieldwork and hostile to love, would move with the familiar beauty of cattle and their hidden pride.

"And put Number Seven up in the loft, or somewhere away from the others. I don't want to see any more of him tonight."

Roberta, whose hands were strong, took Number Seven by his dripping hair and dragged him to his bedroom, groaning a little.

"Oh, how unfair it all is, it really is," said Number Seven as he slid under the single blanket, next to Jean Le Maigre. "Everyone is so bad-tempered here! I'm off. Yes, tomorrow morning."

"So it's you again," Jean Le Maigre said. "And with wet hair on top of everything else! I don't want you in my bed."

But he already had Pomme and Alexis in "his" bed, as well as Number Seven, who was going to have to sleep on the edge because there was so little room.

"I'll have space for myself," said Number Seven. "There'll be room for me and a bed for me when you go to the Noviciat . . ."

"I can't hear you," Jean Le Maigre answered, "I'm asleep." And he gave a jab with his elbow at Pomme, who was sleeping solidly on his plump stomach, and at Alexis, who rolled out as usual onto the floor, snoring the whole time.

"I'm cold," said Number Seven.

"You can get down on your knees and beg me," Jean Le Maigre answered, "but I'm not going to warm you. In any case, I'm already in a deep sleep. I'm dreaming that I'm crossing the river on skates. The river is frozen, but I'm afraid it's going to crack open suddenly. I'm more and more frightened every moment. I am shouting for help! But you don't hear me, you little pig! Get away from me!"

"It's not my fault," Number Seven replied. "I'm on the other side of the river, and anyway, it's not my fault if you dream . . ."

"Quiet," Jean Le Maigre said. "What was I saying just then? You interrupted me at the best part. Ah, yes! I am falling into a hole, the water is icy. I feel sad. There is an eagle flying across the sky. I am drowning. But suddenly a superb line of poetry springs to my lips:

Oh heavens, with a dark goodbye
I . . .

Glug! I don't have time to finish it. I disappear from sight. The waters close over me!

About my frail throat, the strangling hands

Glug! It's all over. I am no longer of this world."

"I'm so cold," said Number Seven in a trembling voice.

"What's making that noise I hear?" Jean Le Maigre asked. "Bears, can it be? Gluggle . . . Gloggle . . . There's a bear outside the house."

"It's Pommes' stomach, you know it is," Number Seven answered.

"The more my stomach shrinks, the bigger his becomes," Jean Le Maigre said. "It's unfair. And on top of that, he lets it burble all night! Come closer, Number Seven, these egotists won't leave us enough room." (Alexis was snoring under the bed, which was sailing along like a schooner.) "We're too good to them, they take advantage of us. Remember that we're better than the rest of the world. I am, anyway. Take off your shirt. It smells horrible. I wonder what Héloïse sleeps in."

"In her convent shift," Number Seven answered, "with her cross on her chest . . . How marvellous it is!"

"It's possible that she sleeps with nothing on at all," Jean Le Maigre said. "You never know."

"Good night," said Number Seven.

Number Seven went right off to sleep. (He was running with Jean Le Maigre through the woods; it was raining, but the sun was still shining between the trees. Jean Le Maigre opened his mouth to drink in the rain. Number Seven thought sadly: "I must reach the orphanage first, because the principal will ask us to conjugate the verb *to lie* and Jean Le Maigre doesn't know how." "It's raining so hard," Jean Le Maigre said, running behind him laughing. "Where are you?" he asked in a clear, suppliant voice . . ."I can't see you any more." "I must get there first," Number Seven thought, "I shall have to answer the principal for him." The bell was already ringing for Mass in the orphanage chapel, and Number Seven was filled with despair as he realized he wouldn't arrive in time . . .)

Number Seven was saying as he opened his eyes, with Jean Le Maigre by his side, doing battle against the lice.

"The lice are eating us alive," Jean Le Maigre said. "Life is impossible."

"If I were you, I'd get some sleep," replied Number Seven (but he himself was afraid of an unwise slumber that might lead him back to the orphanage). "Everyone needs sleep."

"Not me," said Jean Le Maigre. "It's just a waste of time. You know what? I ought to be writing poems."

(Already he could see the title: AN OBSCURE POEM WRITTEN ON MY BROTHER'S BACK DURING HIS BLAMELESS SLEEP.) Number Seven was moving away from him now, skirting the walls of the orphanage, reading the signs the principal was pointing out to him with a cruel finger: THREE DAYS WITHOUT BREAD OR WATER – COUGHING FORBIDDEN – MOVING ABOUT IN BED IS NOT PERMITTED – WE ARE NOT RESPONSIBLE FOR LOST CHILDREN – FOR LICE TAKE THE RIGHT HAND CORRIDOR BUT FIRST REMOVE YOUR SHIRT –

Number Seven was about to choose the Lice Room when he felt Jean Le Maigre's knee sliding between his legs.

"It would be best if we confessed right away, tomorrow morning," Number Seven commented, hurriedly removing his shirt while Jean Le Maigre was pushing Pomme over to the other side of the bed.

"We'd better get on with it quickly before they wake up," Jean Le Maigre said, "those egotists will be so envious otherwise!"

"Now I'm not cold any more," Number Seven said, appreciative of his brother's warm caresses but unable to keep himself from emitting little plaintive "Ows" as he was reminded of the blows that had fallen earlier upon his bruised body, in joy as well as pain, and suddenly: *No, touching my bottom is forbidden,* it's burning like red-hot coals! "Ow . . . ow . . ."

"If you go on whining like a little village virgin," Jean Le Maigre said, "I shall wake up Pomme, at least he doesn't talk at the same time . . ."

"No, don't wake him up," Number Seven said, anxious for Jean Le Maigre to go on all night, to continue his gentle and brutal activities, the careless caresses he constantly broke off to recite poems and tell strange stories, leaving Number Seven to float away on his own, then taking up again where he'd left off, without asking permission. Jean Le Maigre was so familiar with his brother's body that he occasionally forgot it altogether, abruptly turning his back and talking about some other subject. Lying beside his old comrade, neglectful even of his own pleasure, put out by this treatment but still patient, Number Seven either feigned sleep when this happened, or hid his disappointment.

"We'll go and confess as soon as day breaks," Jean Le Maigre said, his mouth already watering at the idea of telling the Curé his sins. "And I shall keep a close watch on you to see that you don't do it again," he went on, "either on your own or with anyone else. Remember, it's a bad habit . . . It must be, because Héloïse doesn't do it, or Grand-mère, or Anita, or Aurelia . . . etc. . . . . It's time you thought about mending your ways, and time I did as well, before my early death. The angels in paradise are going to be very stern with me about it. I shall say that I only did it to warm up a bit, that unfortunately my pitiable brother often led me into temptation, and that all poets have a predilection

for debauchery

"You've never given a thought to my poor soul," Jean Le Maigre continued, pulling Pomme's head toward him as it began to slide out into the void. "You only think of yourself. It's disgusting.

"Yet you haven't been deprived of good examples," he went on, disregarding Number Seven's leg arching tensely against his own. (It's coming nearer and nearer, said Number Seven, in a panting whisper.) "It's not the—" Jean Le Maigre was silent for an instant as Number Seven's last moist caress flowed over his fingers. "Well," Jean Le Maigre then continued, swiftly suppressing a little quiver, "we've managed very well, in spite of the way those two egotists have crowded us. We'll give them their reward. Tomorrow night we'll leave them the whole bed and go under it. Now we must repair the ravages of the cataclysm. We mustn't shock our grandmother with our *awful traces*. Put your shirt back on, and where has mine got to?"

"I do wish I could go to confession right away," Number Seven said, fighting back sleep with difficulty and watching the flames of hell dance on the wall. "Me too," Jean Le Maigre said. "Even at this hour of the night, we ought to go and pay a visit to somebody virtuous: it would bring peace to your soul, and then you wouldn't have to go to hell immediately, during the night. We ought to go and visit Héloïse. She would set us an example, and that would be so good for us."

And leaping out of bed, they did so.

Their visit to Héloïse turned into a novel, which they wrote at dawn, between the bed and the closet, their feet bare in the icy draft that was streaming in through the window, giving them both an earache, a thing from which Jean Le Maigre had suffered greatly in the past but which they finally managed to forget, inflamed as they were by the fine title now inscribed in his exercise book: "Diary of a man being devoured by demons," which Number Seven gazed at raptly, leaning on his brother's shoulder.

"I wish to speak now," wrote Jean Le Maigre, who was collapsing with sleep but did not say so, "of the visit we paid to our sister the saint, who doesn't eat, or steal, or kill, like most people, and whose only company up in her room consists of a *prie-dieu*, a crucifix, and a family of mice that is increasing vastly in numbers every year. The piety of our sister Héloïse is, then, the subject of this sad tale, of which you will read a further chapter every night, at the same hour, if the birds of insomnia torment you as they never fail to torture me! Alas, my brother and I, after a life full of sin, desire to be converted. It is too late, but one always thinks of it too early. And so it was with the intention of converting my brother that I thought of presenting him with the good example provided by our sister – whom I had supposed to be on her knees reciting orisons all through the night, but who, I am ashamed to admit at this point, was not praying at all, quite the contrary. I do not wish to enter into descriptions that might shock my grandmother, who, indiscreet as she is, will certainly read these pages. But my brother and I were very surprised, and happy to be so, when we discovered that our sister was doing on her own what we ourselves like to do together, or with our two brothers when Alexis and Pomme are awake, but they're lazy and prefer to sleep. This incident is of great importance, and I should really devote a chapter to it entitled *The Frustrations of Héloïse* or *The Fall of Héloïse* or *Héloïse Observed One Night at the Moment of Temptation,* but poverty of inspiration now halts my pen

    in its flight

Not only poverty of inspiration but the cold, for the ink is freezing on the end of my pen, and I myself on this cold January night . . ."

"You were writing about Héloïse," Number Seven put in.

"There is an Héloïse mystery," Jean Le Maigre went on, "just as there is a Jean Le Maigre mystery. The reader may follow me in my anguished pil-gri-mage toward death, the forest grows thicker, my eyes begin to close

> *And thinking of my Solitude*
> *I age a thousand years*

I must therefore suspend at this point the pal-pi-tating story of Héloïse. For further details, read next week's instalment. Lifting my eyes from my exercise book, I have just perceived my brother, alas, struck down by sleep and lying there, his face on the floor . . . I myself shall fall upon the floor in a moment or two, and use my brother's elbow as a pillow. I trust that the gentle reader will pardon my absence. My throat is burning, my back is yielding to fatigue, my knees are bending, and from my pain-racked nose . . ."

Jean Le Maigre was asleep.

Jean Le Maigre woke to find himself in a warm bed, supported by a shoulder that turned out to belong to his grandmother, who after stuffing him with honey and rice cakes announced that Monsieur le Curé was waiting downstairs to accompany him to the Noviciat.

"I just won't open my eyes," Jean Le Maigre said, "I shan't move a muscle." (But raising one eyelid, he caught a glimpse of Number Seven laughing in a corner.)

"I shall dress you by force," Grand-mère Antoinette said, dis-entangling Jean Le Maigre's pants from their chair, while Number Seven moved to and fro, bringing his socks, his shoes, his clean shirt, and the slim black necktie that Grand-mère Antoinette always knotted around her grandsons' necks before imprisoning them in the Noviciat for life.

"If I put on that necktie, I'm lost," Jean Le Maigre thought, and disappeared under the bedclothes. "Grand-mère, spare me the dishonour of . . . Spare your child . . . For if I get up it will only be to use your chamberpot, which is under the bed . . ."

"Oh Lord, Lord," Grand-mère Antoinette said, "and he even dares to flout me with that!"

Before she had even had time to exclaim, "Ah, the little villain, the wretch . . ." the thing was done, and Jean Le Maigre was pulling the bedclothes back over his head.

"Help me," Grand-mère said to Number Seven.

And they tugged him out by the feet . . .

Jean Le Maigre allowed himself to be washed, then clothed, without making the slightest effort to help, keeping his arms folded and his head tilted back as though to make it clear that this departure for the Noviciat had nothing to do with him. Number Seven laced up Jean Le Maigre's shoes with an air of great concentration.

"You are not ignorant, dear brother," Jean Le Maigre was saying all the while in solemn tones, "that my grandmother is thrusting me into my grave . . . But I have it in my mind to take my posthumous works with me, and those that are not posthumous as well. Therefore, when you have tied up my socks with string so that they shall not droop and drag behind me like a pair of shattered wings, run to the rescue of my poems, of my novels, of my life work, which is bewailing its fate – poor thing – under every mattress in the house. Run, therefore, to that spot you know of, under the floorboards in the outhouse. And spared thus from my father's vengeance . . ."

Number Seven returned immediately with a pile of manuscripts. These he deposited carefully in Jean Le Maigre's suitcase, asking the author to think of him when he came to write the prefaces.

"The prefaces and the epilogues," said Number Seven, closing the suitcase.

And it was time to go. But so indifferent was Jean Le Maigre to the idea of leaving that he forgot to say goodbye to anyone.

IV

On the back seat (part of the silent harvest Monsieur le Curé had gathered in for the Noviciat – four boys with pale lips and receding chins, whose eyes, hypocritically lowered toward prayer books or rosaries, flashed sudden lying glances . . .), sitting in the car as it slithered and whinnied like an old horse over the icy road, Jean Le Maigre, his cap pulled down over his forehead, his arms folded on his chest, was filled with quiet joy at the idea of belonging to a superior breed. "I," he thought, "enjoy the particular favour of Monsieur le Curé, and in a few years I shall be able to have conversations with the bishops, but they, with their pious manners and their girls' faces, they, those miserable . . ."

"Jean Le Maigre," said Monsieur le Curé, "don't spit on the floor!"

Jean Le Maigre sighed with boredom. Oh Lord, what a trial this is going to be for my brother! He is going to damn himself, he is going to lose his soul now I am gone! His is a weak nature, he loses heart too quickly. I must start thinking now of how to escape. Without me, Number Seven will plunge into drunkenness, he will go and visit women. Oh, my God, what a disaster! And his nights, his long sad nights when I'm not there! Yes, I must escape as soon as I arrive. Tomorrow at the latest, unless there's a moon.

Jean Le Maigre then set about his complicated escape. He was leaping out of the dormitory window (having remembered to strap a great bundle of novels and poems around his waist with his belt), he was just falling painfully on to his knees in the courtyard, when Monsieur le Curé said in a gruff voice, *Everyone out to push the car!* But though the four saints immediately flung themselves out on the road to push the car, Jean Le Maigre and Monsieur le Curé did not move from their seats. They sat discussing the rigours of the climate as they drank a bottle of beer.

"It's simply a question of the engine," Monsieur le Curé explained. "It just can't take the cold. You have to stop and warm it up, and then brrum . . . brrum . . . you're off again. There! You see!"

The four Little Brothers ran along beside them and tumbled back into the car.

"It's nothing," Monsieur le Curé said. "It often stops like that, but one always gets there in the end . . . And now, which way? Ah, yes! To the south still . . ."

There were several stops of a similar nature. Once, while driving south, they found themselves pointing north in the middle of a field.

"An effort, we must make a big effort this time," Monsieur le Curé said.

And dragging Jean Le Maigre behind him, he got out and sank into the snow up to his knees. ("It's a question of weight, I'm too heavy. Help me, Jean Le Maigre, that's it, that's the way, and now, whatever can the time be? We must get there before it grows dark. Blow your nose, Jean Le Maigre, it's running like a sugar maple. Then we must decide how we're to get out of here.")

Jean Le Maigre considered Monsieur le Curé's ears.

"Not on your sleeve," Monsieur le Curé added. "With this handkerchief!"

"His ears are really very impressive," Jean Le Maigre thought, "and think of all the sins they've tracked down and nailed! The finest sins in the world have been poured into them. Gluttony, lust, avarice, pride. Ah! Pride, straight as an arrow, and envy, sinuous as a snake." Then, as he bent to pick up Monsieur le Curé's beret, whipped off his head yet again by the wind (Your beret Monsieur le Curé . . .): "What a beautiful bald head," he thought, "I am impressed by the wisdom it must contain. Since I am a constant victim of lice, perhaps I should cut off all my hair this evening. A beautiful bald head! That would make my brother respect me for my learning, but I shall never have a paunch like Monsieur le Curé's, I'd better give up that idea right away . . ."

Supporting Monsieur le Curé, carried along with him, enmeshed in the eddies of his cassock, Jean Le Maigre passed through the iron gates of the Noviciat. He had had so much to drink, to keep warm from one village to the next, that he was scarcely able to stay upright on his long wobbly legs. He let the Little Brothers file in first, their ears red with the cold, shivering in their lightweight coats. But Jean Le Maigre felt his head full of fire, his heart of joy. He was thinking of his imminent escape.

"It is a late vocation," Monsieur le Curé explained, "but it is not hopeless. Take care of his lungs and shave his head. He's being eaten alive by lice. He's dirty outside, but a good washing will let some light into his soul." Jean Le Maigre approved these sentiments with a wide, humble, somewhat hypocritical smile. "I might perhaps wait till tomorrow to escape," he thought, tempted by the smell of meat broth wafting out from the kitchens, where he could hear the hum of the other students' voices. "They will have some respect for my intelligence here. There are a great many devotional books. I shall become pious without even knowing it, I shall be able to lecture everyone about virtue. I shall have visions, the saints will speak to me in my sleep, and the angels, ah! the angels

> *With gold and flowers*
> *Shall crown my brow*

Yes. Yes! I want to be converted right away, and renounce my former idleness forever." All the same, Jean Le Maigre grew sad as he thought that, even as they were hanging around his neck, under his black necktie (already so symbolic of the mourning in his soul), a heavy medallion that clanged like a death knell against his frail chest. (And was the principal not telling him, as he exhaled his foul breath into his face, that he must renounce, renounce forever all the goods and temptations of this world? . . .) Yes, he thought, as all this was happening, Pomme and Number Seven are drinking in the cellar as usual, or telling each other's fortunes with the cards, in the candlelight . . . But how consoling, too, the image of them held captive by evening prayers, each pinned by his sleeve to Grand-mère Antoinette's skirt . . .

Or then again, the image of them both, one after the other, with their pants off in a corner, waiting for their daily thrashing . . . These thoughts brought him comfort as he made his way into the Refectory, preceded by the four Little Brothers walking with lowered eyes.

7 o'clock – Prayers

8 o'clock – Meditation

8:30 – Prayers

9 o'clock – Examination of Conscience

Jean Le Maigre glanced over the Noviciat timetable pinned up on the notice board in the corridor, and found himself already making responses to the crystalline *Ave* being recited by one of the tiny, melancholy voices at his side . . .

That evening, and every other evening, Jean Le Maigre ate molasses, then more molasses. They ate it on bread, on their solitary midday omelettes – they ate it at every meal. Jean Le Maigre ate ferociously, like everyone around him, listening with quivering ears to the life of Saint X (filled, by the way, with tortures that Jean Le Maigre approved of, his nose buried in his bowl of milk so as not to miss a single drop), read by the priest standing up on the dais. Jean Le Maigre himself intended to write, for the edification of his comrades, the life of a saint who had become a sinner. *They stoned him and tortured him till dawn* . . . The blood flowed in streams over the tabletop, and Jean Le Maigre sopped it up with his handkerchief. Then he went on eating, his hand slipping from one plate to another, stealing food from the boys sitting next to him.

A lament arose suddenly in the silent evening air . . . All the doors and all the windows seemed to be banging in the wind. As he tried to pull his fingers out of the sticky molasses, Jean Le Maigre felt the winter winds streaming in through the holes in his boots. The novices were all holding their breath, their knives held pointed into the air, wild-eyed as they waited for the death of the Holy Victim they did not dare to kill themselves. *Silence silence at last* Jean Le Maigre closed his eyes. He breathed out gently in his turn. A clamour of relief filled the hall. And Jean Le Maigre suddenly heard the grumbling cries of his stomach sounding in his ears.

"Silence!" the priest cried, and closed his book.

Jean Le Maigre gave a smile of satisfaction, a smile that was shared by all his comrades as they laid down their knives obediently upon the tables.

"I feel good all of a sudden," Jean Le Maigre thought. "I could fly up to heaven, if my stomach didn't feel so heavy. I am good," he thought, "I no longer have wicked thoughts. What I need now is a really good vision to impress everyone with . . ."

And it was thus that the Devil began to appear to Jean Le Maigre, cautiously at first, then more and more often. He came in through the dormitory windows, stepping out of the moonlight, wearing his black robe, his fur hat down over his forehead, his muddy shoes held in his hand. Jean Le Maigre made haste to finish his Examination of Conscience before the Devil finally slipped into his bed. It was midnight, the assistant master was already snoring in his cubicle, but under his door there still flowed a trickle of red light in which the sleepwalkers, wandering from bed to bed, dabbled their feet as in a pool. Buried in their stiff nightshirts, exhaling a chorus of laments, some lay in a blessed sleep, their hands clasped on the bedclothes, their noses sticking straight up in the air, like so many drowned corpses floating on the water. Others awakened temptations by moving about in their beds, for, as the supervisor said: *When the beds creak, I know what is happening,* and he was right. Jean Le Maigre himself, sweating with fever in his cotton shirt, had in a very few nights gone through every bed in the dormitory. He consoled himself by thinking of Pomme and Number Seven, for they, at least, were sleeping the sleep of innocence under their grandmother's wing.

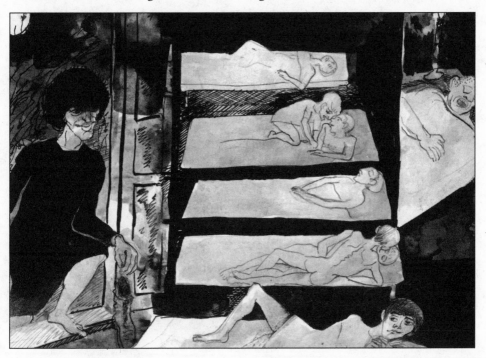

Seen by the light of day, the Devil was none other than Frère Théo-dule, who had been relegated to the task of administering the Infirmary when he was not giving classes in natural science to rows of dozing students. "You're getting thinner," Frère Théodule would say cheerfully as Jean Le Maigre stepped on the weighing machine. "You're getting thinner all the time." His feet bared to the cold draft, Jean Le Maigre drank warm milk and thought that the time had come for him to write his will to Number Seven and choose the spot where his grandmother was to bury him.

"Warm milk every morning," Frère Théodule said, placing a moist hand on Jean Le Maigre's shoulder, "warm milk every evening. And don't get your feet wet."

Jean Le Maigre coughed, then spat blood, constantly encouraged by Frère Théodule, who wiped the corners of his mouth with a handkerchief or watched him faint with passionate admiration. Jean Le Maigre was beautiful when he fainted. He looked like those other young souls that Frère Théodule had precipitated into the life eternal at such a tender age: Narcisse, who died at thirteen years and six months; Brother Paul, who departed this life on his twelfth birthday . . . Frère Théodule was young and loved youth. Still in love with the flower of adolescence, he plucked it as it passed, when he had the time.

Jean Le Maigre appreciated the fact that the Noviciat was one of those strange gardens in which, as elsewhere, the graceful plants of Vice and Virtue grow with stems inextricably intertwined. Nailed to his bed now, by the doctor's orders and Frère Théodule's solicitous complicity, Jean Le Maigre was ruefully writing his autobiography . . .

From the day I was born, I have worn a crown of lice on my head! A poet, my father cried, in a burst of joy. Grand-mère, a poet! They approached my cradle and gazed down at me in silence. My gaze glowed already with a dark and tormented fire. My eyes sent flames of genius shooting all through the room. How beautiful he is, my mother said, how fat, and how good he smells! What a pretty mouth! What a fine brow! I yawned in vanity, and with good reason. A brow crowned with lice and surrounded by garbage! Oh, sad world! Returning from the fields through the kitchen door, the fat-cheeked Muses cut off the sight of the sky from me with their sun-blackened backs. Ah! how I wept as I touched my bald head . . .

I cannot think of my life without having ink flow in abundant streams from my impatient pen. (Tuberculos Tuberculorum, what a wretched destiny for a boy as gifted as thou art, Oh skinny Jean, thou whose feet have been nibbled by rats . . .)

Pivoine is dead
Pivoine is dead
Time for dinner everyone

But, happily, Pivoine had died the evening before, thus yielding his place to me with the utmost consideration. My poor brother had been carried off by the epi . . . api . . . the apocalypse . . . the epilepsy, I mean, several hours before my birth, which allowed everyone to indulge in a good meal with Monsieur le Curé after the funeral service.

Pivoine returned to the earth without complaint, and I sprang from it howling. But not only did I howl, my mother howled too, with pain, and to cover the noise of our howls, my father gaily slaughtered a pig in the cowshed! What a day! The blood flowed in abundance, and in his little black box under the earth Pivoine (Joseph-Aimé) slept peacefully, and thought of us all no more.

"One more angel up in heaven," Monsieur le Curé said. "God must love you to punish you like that!"

My mother shook her head. "But Monsieur le Curé, that's the second in a year."

"Ah, but think how God has rewarded you," Monsieur le Curé replied. Monsieur le Curé admired me from that day forward. I was the reward! How they had waited for me! How they had longed for me! How they needed me! I arrived at exactly the right time to bring my parents joy. A blessing sent from heaven, Monsieur le Curé said.

He is green he is green
Mother, God is going to take him from us
This one as well

"Héloïse," Monsieur le Curé said, "eat in peace, my child." Little Héloïse had wept a great deal on Pivoine's grave, and her eyes were still red.

"She is too sensitive," Monsieur le Curé said, stroking her head. "She must go to the convent."

"But he is so green," Héloïse said, twisting around in her chair to get a better look at me. "As green as celery," she added.

Monsieur le Curé had seen the miraculous sign upon my brow.

"Who knows, perhaps a future vocation? Long ears, so he will be intelligent. Very intelligent."

"The important thing is that he should be able to milk cows and chop wood," my father said curtly.

"Joseph-Aimé is dead, Joseph-Aimé is dead," said my mother, and blew her nose very loudly.

"Console yourself with thoughts of the future," Monsieur le Curé said to her. "Don't look behind you. This child will blush red before he commits his first mortal sin, I promise you. And talking of sins, and I know something about these things, this child, God forgive him, will commit many, many of them."

Not only did I almost die of my greenness, but Number Seven inherited it when he was born. Dig his grave, my grandmother said, already divining the meningitis galloping behind that ill-favoured brow, by turns yellow, grey, and green, and topped by a random scattering of red bristles, like aggressive thorns. "If it's not meningitis, then it's scarlet fever, but either way the child is not going to come out of it alive."

"God's blessing is upon large families," Monsieur le Curé told them as he made haste to baptize Number Seven before the malady carried him off unhallowed, like the unfortunate Joseph-Aimé. "There are some trials that are also benisons, Fortuné-Mathias, may the impure spirit now depart from you . . ."

And it departed from him on the spot. To the great disappointment of my grandmother, who had already made her preparations for the funeral and chosen a black dress in which to mourn the child, Number Seven came back to life. Revived by the baptismal water, his red hair standing upright on his head, Number Seven began to emit such piercing screams that my father came running in from the barn.

"Lord," my father said as he beheld this bristle-haired monster, "this idiot child has made me lose my cow . . ."

My mother wiped away her tears. Never mind, my grandmother said, we'll have a funeral some other time; there are always people dying. Ah, how piously I sprouted up beneath my grandmother's skirt in those far-off days! . . . I was virtuous and always closed my eyes during prayers so as to be like Héloïse, whose ardent piety my grandmother never failed to praise, on Sundays, when she spoke to Monsieur le Curé. I played at saying Mass in summer, and at funerals in winter: Héloïse would bury me up to the neck in snow. It was in this way that I began to cough and waste away. Colds and bouts of pneumonia fell upon me like so many maledictions. I never stopped blowing my nose: on my grandmother's petticoats, on Héloïse's apron. I sneezed like a duck. But everyone in the house was coughing; you could hear the coughs rustling like a dry wind through every crack in the beds and doors.

"It's only during the winter," my father said, and he was right. When spring came, we all began to bud and bloom with lice and measles. That was the time when Number Seven was just beginning to walk, his belly bare under his checked waistcoat, smiling and dribbling at everyone, his head swollen with pride. Ah, if I had but known the hidings that awaited me on his account!

Yet my grandmother had warned me. "Beware of that monster with the red hair," she said that very first day. "He has already deceived everyone with that meningitis of his. Dead, he ought to be dead, and look at that. A caterpillar, he moves like a caterpillar!"

"A bad influence, an evil companion," Monsieur le Curé would say (touching my forehead with his rough hand) on Sunday mornings, "that Fortuné has a thick skin: he doesn't cry when you thrash him!"

Abandoned by our poor mother, who, when she was not in the fields or in the stable taking care of her consumptive mare (the smell of which was not unlike my own now, I must admit), would hold conversations with her dead, all of them lined up side by side on the old harmonium gnawed by rats (our only inheritance from Grand-père Napoléon, who liked to play hymns at night to drive my chaste grandmother into a rage). The November dead, the dead who had died on long winter evenings – my mother called them up, one by one, from the shadows where they were comfortably snoring, and standing there in her pale mauve nightgown, a few sparse hairs falling over her ever humid brow, that sad woman gazed with gentle eyes upon the children, the babies with their toothless smiles, that row of aging photographs she had communed with a thousand times . . .

Ah! she would falter out, imploringly, Hector, why did you desert me? Can you hear me? Gemma! Gemma! You were scarcely one day old when you went away. Can you hear me, Gemma?

As the hours went by, the various names and all those different lives became confused in my mother's mind: the dead began a bewildering waltz before her eyes. (She thought of Gemma, but without knowing it she was seeing a picture of Olive instead, of Olive's tiny bleeding skull crushed beneath my father's plough. And Gemma? Ah! The day of her First Communion! Yes, vanished forever, just like that, in her white lace dress!)

Gemma, Barthélèmy, Léopold. She still had some woollen bootees belonging to that far-off Barthélèmy, whom she was no longer quite certain she remembered giving birth to, but no matter! And Léopold, one year, only one more year and he would have graduated from the Seminary. Léopold, who was so very gifted! Ah!

God had taken Léopold in a curious fashion. By the hair, as one might pull a carrot from the ground.

Returning from a jovial day's butchering of rabbits and foxes, the elder brothers found hanging in the branches of a solitary tree, who do you think? The skeleton-like form of Léopold in his seminarist's cassock, swaying in the wind, dead, very dead, ready for skinning with the rest of the bag they were clutching in their triumphant hands. Lord in heaven, they sighed in chorus, *what a thing to do on Good Friday!* I have always thought he must have had some very black ideas in his head, that one! But drunk with their hunting, with the beer they had consumed, and with the wind lashing at their temples, the elder brothers untied Léopold from the tree. (I should add at this point that Léopold was so brilliant that at the age of ten he could recite by heart whole passages from the Bible he did not understand in the slightest, and also that he could write epitaphs in Latin . . . I have myself inherited the same adventurous spirit as my brother, and, like him, I shall leave behind me relics destined to perish in the dust, *the dust of time,* if you like – for apart from the dear Curé, and Frère Théodule, who is at this very moment forcing me to submit to the ordeal of his thermometer, who is there to read my Latin prose?)

And so, having untied Léopold from his tree, the elder brothers threw him over their shoulders like a sack of potatoes and returned light-heartedly home, where they laid out their bag for us to see, including dear Léopold with his rope belt still around his neck.

"Malediction! Oh! Malediction!" my father cried, and spat upon ground. My mother alone shed the tears of mourning so comforting to Léopold.

Abandoned then (as I was saying) by our mother, wandering orphans with faces covered with daubs of soup, and bottoms of red hot from our father's belt (this was the time when Héloïse made the soup, and never stopped shrieking out as she stood on her chair: "Mother! Mother! The cat is in the soup!"), Fortuné and I began our descent to hell. Tragically scarred by the example of our brother Léopold, we made many suicide attempts, none of which were ultimately successful, for Héloïse always managed to betray us with a joyful cry before whoever's turn it was had crossed the threshold of eternity. "Mother, Mother, the bread knife, Mother, Oh! he's bleeding, Mother!" There was the temptation by water (how good it felt, throwing oneself into the well in summer and being fished out again by the braces of one's pants, clutched in my grandmother's ever watchful hand!) and then the temptation by fire. We started fires everywhere, contemptible, idle creatures that we were. My grandmother had scarcely finished making a pair of curtains out of her sheets when we were watching them go up in flames. They flamed deliciously, I might add, and for the first time in my life I had a feeling of achievement. My father was obliged to send us to school, being unable to take a pair of incendiaries like us out into his already barren fields . . . *After school, listen all you women, after school they go to the reformatory!*

My mother complained that life was hard, and men cruel.

"I don't want to hear another word," my father said, *"I'm smoking!"*

He was smoking indeed, and the smell his pipe spread through the house was the smell of all our family corpses . . . But Number Seven and I had the greatest respect for father's *smoking hour.* Each sitting at one end of the table, hands on our knees, our reading primers scattered on the floor (what a wretched thing it is, learning to read, after all; my grandmother was the first to learn), but our minds still full of the echoing *ba's* and *boo's, bee's, bin's, bun's,* and *bow's* that we had scanned with such perfunctory glances on the blackboard at school (ah, dear old school, forever threatening collapse before the onslaughts of wind and snow; and the tiny flame in the stove that kept us warm, though never to excess . . .), we watched the smoke stream out and turn into that sequence of giant letters, the O's, the L's, and the C's (and also a few musical notes), that our father formed with his unlettered mouth, our father who could not so much as read his own name, even printed in capital letters. In this way our father sat writing novels and stories that he would never read, for from his pipe there rose the misty illustrations of my future works. It was thus that I became a poet. The solemn decision was taken that very night, as I sat with Fortuné in the outhouse, sharing a bench that hugged our buttocks with a pleasant warmth, extracted from it by a system of exchange, and at a high rate of interest. My father was not the only one who smoked; the elder brothers too, seated around my father, their legs stretched out in their blue overalls, wriggling their toes in their woollen socks (which they took off only once every six months, and even then only for the sake of my grandmother's health), breathed delicate and sensuous sighs of smoke that expired in their beards, or even an occasional *Eh* or *Oh*, and sometimes tiny yawns that looked like flies. But the fact was, as I always complained in my precocious wisdom: they hadn't the imagination to say anything else. Thus Number Seven and I, it goes without saying, were superior to everyone else. It is true that our schoolteacher, Mlle Lorgnette, had good reason to complain of our behaviour to Monsieur le Curé.

"Monsieur le Curé, they are little . . . little . . ."

"Hoodlums," Monsieur le Curé put in. "I have known them from their cradles. I am particularly mistrustful of the one with red hair. But the other commits only venial sins. He is good, sensitive, intelligent . . ."

Mlle Lorgnette was reassured.

Ah, her legs turning blue with the cold! The legs of Mlle Lorgnette! Ah, her long eyelashes!

> *They were the first shadows*
> *That passion ever cast on me*

I was so in love that I could no longer sleep. Adoringly, Mlle Lorgnette would deck my waistcoat buttonhole with medals and decorations, the Ribbon of the Association of Prize Pupils – though unfortunately I was the sole member of the Association, for Number Seven never came to school except to snatch a little sleep, and Pomme only to eat the licorice that Mlle Lorgnette always gave him, together with a warm seat near the stove.

"Only the best students are allowed near the stove," she would say, "and only the worst ones are allowed to sleep."

Thanks to a system of exchange involving his licorice sticks and a choice of places at night – *on the bed under the bed or across the bed* – Pomme always ended up next to the stove, the movements of his plump stomach varying according to the intensity of the flames. (Number Seven and I always kept the best places at night.) Mlle Lorgnette herself frequently missed school. Like Number Seven, she would wander off among the snowdrifts, losing her toque in the wind and sucking at the ice that formed on the thumbs of her mittens. Occasionally I took the class for her; at other times, Monsieur le Curé himself, having escaped from all the old maids in his confessional, would appear in the doorway, an imposing figure with his geography maps tucked under his arm.

At such times I would always run out to meet him with zealous haste, help him to remove his coat, and brush the snowflakes from his bald head. What a pleasure it was for me to gaze and gaze again at that shining scalp, as bare as a smooth white stone!

"Jean Le Maigre," Monsieur le Curé would say, "I sometimes wonder what I should do without you. By the by, my son, Bernadine passed away last night. Yes, yes! I am now without a servant. May God keep her soul! She went sleepwalking and caught a chill in the snow, then phtt! Well, I always thought she was none too sound in the head. Always mixing pepper up with the sugar, you know, and worse still, sugar with the mustard. She drank my consecrated wine as well, in secret. Ah, yes! Things like that . . . Well, there I was, asleep, my legs nice and warm by the fire, my soul at peace after the good meal she had just cooked for me . . . telling myself all the same, in my sleep, *Monsieur le Curé you have drunk too much beer again* . . . again! And all that while, my Bernardine, ah, God keep her soul! It was a sad end. She was virtue itself, you know – so modest she would lower her eyes when a man took off his shoes. But what can I do, I must find myself another servant, I'm such an old cripple, you see! But in the meantime let us venture forth across the seas, my child . . ."

Monsieur le Curé opened the door on an empty classroom. A cat crouching in one corner lifted one eye, then dropped it again immediately. Pomme was licking his stick of licorice.

"I'll come back again tomorrow," Monsieur le Curé said. "What a disgrace!"

But then, the second after, "No," Monsieur le Curé added, "let us profit from the absence of the ignorant by doing a little geography."

I warmed myself with a course of instruction on Morocco. Monsieur le Curé and I had a preference for warm climates and for even numbers. When the geography lesson was over, Monsieur le Curé taught me Greek (which caused me to remember the astonishing history of my brother Léopold, and I tried to make him tremble with stupefaction in his grave). "You are too ambitious," Monsieur le Curé said. "You are too fond of competition. Beware of pride, my child. It could lead you to hell." Monsieur le Curé also taught me how to spell, and the rudiments of astronomy, for, he pointed out, *you must have silver moons stars and a stormy sky* in all your poems. "Ah! I was forgetting," he then said, "East, West, and South . . . It would be as well for you to have some idea where they are. I have never been sure myself, and my hair is now white." (White hair? Yes, a single one; I saw it suddenly, sprouting behind his ear.) "I am not to blame," Monsieur le Curé said. "It is the fault of my car, yes, my car in its fury is to blame. You know it, it is a prey to frenzy when set in motion, I never know whither it will lead me. And that, may God forgive me, is the reason why dying members of my flock are cheated of their last rites from time to time. But, Horace, ah, he always waits for me: a fine fellow, a noble old man! *Well well here is Monsieur le Curé come to visit me,* he says when he sees me arriving at last, all out of breath, my prayer book in my hand. *What a surprise, eh? I ought really to get up* . . . He is deaf, but he can always tell what his curé says to him. Horace, I say to him, don't move, for this time I greatly fear . . .

"No, no, he replies, it won't be today, Monsieur le Curé. I'll bet you one of my calves that it isn't today . . .

"No bargaining on the brink of death, Horace. I've told you that a hundred times. But I would be willing to accept one of your sheep, one of the very young ones . . .

"How would I feed my poor without him?

"And next time you'll make it your coat of wildcat fur, eh Horace?

"How would I clothe my poor without him?"

Horace weathered the storm, received Extreme Unction, and decided not to expire: and thus Monsieur le Curé was able to clothe his poor. One February morning Grand-mère Antoinette came back from five o'clock Mass swathed in Horace's fur coat, scorching us all with the proud lightning of her gaze, so that I could no longer tell which was the ferocious animal – the wildcat coat or my grandmother in her splendour.

Jealous, my father decided to go to five o'clock Mass himself every morning from then on, and declared loudly to my grandmother that she could give shelter to a whole *caravan of animals beneath that coat of woe!*

"At last you have spoken a word of good sense," my grandmother answered, already sheltering Anita and one or another of the little A's beneath her mountainous folds of fur.

The five o'clock Mass did my father a great deal of harm, and we all became victims once more, each in our turn, of the cold draft of his ill temper. Despite his many efforts, Monsieur le Curé was never able to instruct me in the all-important verities of life. I never knew where the East was, North even less, and I always felt that the West was wandering around the house, with its head down, like someone who is bored.

"But there is no hurry," Monsieur le Curé said, "one always gets there in the end . . ."

Heaped with pictures of the Virgin by Mlle Lorgnette, rewarded with continuously brilliant marks, I paid much less attention to my *behaviour and morals.* These, like the temperature, sometimes dipped below zero. *Little brute little pest wicked scamp,* Mlle Lorgnette whispered in my ear. I stored up these words of love lovingly within me. There were also a great many more that it would be futile to write down here, for the list would be too long, and increasingly risqué. And I fear that Frère Théodule (at present busy making medicines, poisons, and glue in his laboratory) may come and read this over my shoulder, as he is ever tempted to do whenever he sees me, pen in hand, spreading a rainbow of ink around me, on the wall, on the bedclothes . . . ("That's it! That's it, my child!" Frère Théodule says. "It is the last great flash of energy before the end") in a sad and solitary apothi . . . tho . . . apotheosis!

Frère Théodule would not be pleased if he were to find out how great an influence Mlle Lorgnette had on my life. She was, after all, only a few years older than me, and I would soon be a whole Greek-filled head taller than she. (Proud as a turkey cock, I had been leaving my Greek prose, my funeral orations, my fables, and my tragedies lying around all over the house for some time before I discovered that my father had consigned them to the latrines as fast as I could write them. What a disappointment! That was the state to which I was reduced by my father's cruelty and my grandmother's passion for thrift, which would not allow anything to go to waste, be it string or Greek prose.) Though Mlle Lorgnette sometimes exclaimed at the extent of my learning, she was also becoming more and more dejected at the limitations of her own.

"I'm afraid I need your help," she told me one day during a private conversation . . ."I would like to know how you spell the following words: *elefant forrage allementary and incrongrous.*"

I didn't know either *incrongrous* or *allementary*, and I wore out my eyes going through the only dictionary in the school, which went only as far as the letter H, on page 122. Mlle Lorgnette was obliged to lend me her spectacles, for my sight became steadily poorer as the daylight faded.

"The Inspector of Schools has promised me a lamp, an oil lamp. Yes, we shall have it before next Christmas."

Meantime I was wandering through the darker vales of learning, and drinking in such words as *crocodiles concholgoy concentrically.*

"That's enough," Mlle Lorgnette said when I uttered the word *conception*, and accompanied it with a cry of : "At least I know what that means!"

"That's enough," she said. "You may leave now, I don't need you any more. I am *enlightened very enlightened* good evening." Saying which, she pushed me slowly toward the door, tapping me on the fingers with her pointer.

"That will teach me to keep you after school! Oh, you wicked scamp! . . ."

Naturally Mlle Lorgnette accused me unjustly once again of attempting to embrace her. It was dark by then, how could I have seen her mouth?

Being too young to understand my passion, Number Seven was meanwhile wandering over the hills, begging in the villages. He smoked a great deal and choked me with his poisonous breath at night. Fortuné was graduating from commerce to mendacity. He sold his bootlaces on street corners, and my grandmother had not a single button left on her coat. This was because Number Seven, if he hadn't eaten them, as I suspected him of doing, had bartered them to one of the drunks in the neighbourhood for a bottle of cider. *That boy will bring shame upon us!* my grandmother said when she discovered that Number Seven, in the course of empty-ing the loft, was preparing to sell Grand-père Napoléon's crutches and the cassock Léopold had worn at the Seminary. *He will come to no good,* my father declared, his head buried in his beard. Number Seven smoked anything, being unable to distinguish between his brothers' pipes and the tobacco he obtained from local drunkards and rolled into cigarettes with pages from his arithmetic book. We only had one arithmetic book for the whole class, and it was thus that I was forever deprived of the answer to my problem:

$$100 + 148 - 142 + 10000000 - 3 \times 20 \times 10$$

Ah! Number Seven had no self-respect! And that was to be my downfall. On his days off, when he was not involved in bargaining for chickens or other livestock, Number Seven used to come to school. He surprised Mlle Lorgnette a great deal by his attention to her arithmetic classes and indeed to everything even remotely connected with financial gain. The numbers would be firmly fixed in his head almost before he'd learned them. Perhaps it was because he was so used to stealing other people's money. Or else he was already being gnawed away inside by avarice. As a consequence of his familiarity with all the good-for-nothings in the village, my brother used to tell dirty stories more and more. He would blaspheme until he was out of breath, egged on by the wide black laughter (all their teeth were rotten like mine) of the Elder Brothers. Fortuné used to share the mouldy bread, alas, of those whom Monsieur le Curé referred to in his sermons as the black sheep of his flock, *his lepers his incurable drinkers his corrupted children with tender hearts.* "Yes, yes, come unto me, my house is always open, but I beg of you not to come into God's house when in a state of drunkenness!" Fortuné, in short, was already drinking the bitter wine of depravity. Though still too small to venture into taverns, he drank wherever and whenever the generosity of his friends permitted it (And what friends! They ran the whole gamut, from Coco the Stiff to Martin the Killer), using the same little tin cup from which he ate his soup in the evenings, at home. How sad it was, oh Lord! As for myself, I only drank once a week, on Friday evening, before appearing to hear my father's weekly verdict (yes, Friday night was punishment night, and it was as well to prepare oneself for the verdict several days in advance), and sometimes on Wednesdays too, when, devoured by my own uneasiness, I waited for Mlle Lorgnette on the school porch. Chaste laments would swell in my breast as I imagined how, at that very instant perhaps, Mlle Lorgnette was experiencing with horror the cruel claws of a wolf tearing at her breast . . .

"I'm not afraid of wolves," Mlle Lorgnette said, when she joined me on the porch, at a late hour. "I am perfectly capable of defending myself. You can go now. Good night."

Then I remembered that I had had too much to drink. There were strange things stirring in my entrails, as ships shudder before the final wreck.

"Heavens, how pale you are, my child! Is something wrong? Has something terrible happened to your father?"

"He is very well, mademoiselle, alas, yes, he is healthier than ever, he's putting on weight. Oh! Can I sit down beside you, mademoiselle? Can I lie down on your desk? I feel weak, very weak."

"No one may get up on my platform," mademoiselle replied with a shake of her chignon, "unless it be the Inspector General of Schools when he visits us next Christmas. Always remember that, my child. You must get ready to go now. The class is over."

But she opened up her desk, yes, and my nostrils quivered with gratitude. (No, no, do not get up on my platform; stay there below. There must always be a certain distance between the student and the teacher. Remember that, for the future. I want to be proud of my students when the Inspector General of Schools comes to see us. Perhaps you will be the only one in school that day, in which case it is as well that you should learn good manners, so that the Inspector may disregard the absence of my other charges. One first-class student means more to me than a whole benchful of bad students fast asleep. Remember that too, my friend. Goodbye for now. I must correct all your papers. I must prepare my lessons for tomorrow.)

"You expect too much attention, Jean Le Maigre. I can't give all my time to you. Off you go, now. Go take care of your cold. Good night." Ah! That smell of licorice from Mlle Lorgnette's desk! With a swift gesture, she slipped a licorice stick into my mouth. "Go now . . . go . . . now . . ." She continued to push me toward the door. But suddenly, what a disaster, I threw up a lakeful of beer (But whatever have you been eating? Sardines? Chalk?) onto the wall, adding another river to the map of the world.

"Monsieur le Curé will be very upset," Mlle Lorgnette said. "He intended to take us on a trip to Rome tomorrow. He will be very disappointed," she added sadly. And then, soberly: "All we have left is my pencil, my desk, and the stove. The Inspector General of Schools will reprimand me again. Our school is falling to pieces."

Feeling my throat constricted with emotion, and also by an intense desire to throw up, I politely apologized to Mlle Lorgnette, and a long tear trickled very slowly down my cheek.

"It's nothing," Mlle Lorgnette replied. "Monsieur le Curé is goodhearted, you can leave now. I forgive you. But remember the respect you owe me. Good night." And opening the door, she thrust me forth into the tempest.

I never saw Mlle Lorgnette again. She left the school before the Inspector's visit. And to please Mlle Lorgnette, I have never again stepped up on a school platform.

Mlle Lorgnette was replaced by the Widow Casimir, a flourishing widow built like a tower, with the generous curves of a pitcher and breasts in full bloom behind a rampart of pins and knitting needles. Mme Casimir was waiting to find a husband. Waiting had put creases in her eyelids and rubbed off her smile. Indeed, I suspected this woman of having a hard heart, for she never raised her eyes from her knitting, and did not know how to conjugate the verb *absolve*. I absolve . . . you absolve . . . he . . . ab . . . and there she stopped, pointer hovering in the air. She also had a mania for confusing words containing the syllable *vest*, such as *vestibule* and *vestry*; and she would say to me in harsh tones, *Go and divest yourself in the divestry, young man!* Which was a source of humiliation to me, for the vestibule was an open field. Little by little, I lost my interest in geography and decided to turn my mind, as my brother had done, to trade. I went to school in the morning, then spent the afternoon

selling barrels, chains, and axes stolen from old Horace's barn. In
the evening, escaping from our grandmother and her rosary, we
made our majestic way down to the cellar and counted the pennies
we had made. They were few in number, but we loved to watch
them glitter in the flickering candlelight.

As he grew older, Number Seven began to take an increasing
interest in women. The little girls were appreciative of the way he
lifted up their skirts on the way to Communion. Particularly
Marthe, the little hunchback who sat on the same bench with me
at school. Marthe loved us both equally, and we both had an equal
admiration for her fingernails, which she painted red, or orange, or
pink. Furthermore, she could make plum tarts, and also rhubarb
jam. After Mlle Lorgnette's departure, Pomme came to school very
rarely. The absence of licorice and caramels in Mme Casimir's desk
was a great trial to him. His stomach began to get flatter, and there

was more and more room in our bed at night. Marthe's arrival at school gave back to Pomme the feeling of security he so badly needed. Bloated with bread and butter, he could be heard snoring once more beside the stove. And Number Seven and I had the time to cover Marthe's fat, moist cheeks with kisses, while Mme Casimir counted her stitches . . . Pwfuh . . . Pwfuh . . .

"What is that strange sound I hear?" Mme Casimir would say as she lifted her eyes from her knitting. "A tiny little noise . . ."

Marthe's kisses were noisy and disturbing – so noisy that Pomme always woke up and interrupted us. My mood would suddenly darken as I thought that love could never last.

Mme Casimir did not feel the cold. Protected as she was by the storm windows of her corset, by the rampart of her breasts, she could never be pierced by the arrows of the cold. In December she said that it was warm in class, in February she spoke of opening a window. What misery for our bare elbows as they poked through the holes they had worn in our sleeves. The damp branches we collected in the woods on the way to school produced only a delicate and slender tongue of flame that went out again as soon as it was lit.

"We must light a fire," Number Seven kept saying, "we must light a fire." So obsessed was he by the cold that he even talked in his sleep about stealing the votive candles from the church and using them to warm up the school. His nightmares were full of red-hot coals and darting flames. We were moving on into deep winter, and the cold was ravaging our hearts.

"We must have a fire," said Number Seven, his eyes glittering in a disquieting way beneath his red shock of hair, "we must have a fire." That same evening he set fire to the school. In my despair I helped him a little.

"If you love me," Marthe said, "set fire to the whole school, just to give me pleasure."

Ah! Ah, God, and to think I heeded her! But I did try to save the dais, and Mlle Lorgnette's desk, oh yes! . . . But Mlle Lorgnette's desk perished with the school, and several days later, after our father had meted out a punishment commensurate with the deed, we left for the Reformatory, our bundles on our backs. In his innocence, Number Seven compared himself to Martin the Killer, climbing the scaffold of rebellion step by step, clenching his fists ever tighter inside his pockets, and raking the landscape as we passed with a savage gaze, his eyes brimming bright with pride and fear. Dreaming of a triumphant entry into the *Home for Lost Children,* we were extremely disappointed by the welcome given us by the Director (a brute, a satyr, a real monster!), who shut us up in the dark, in *cell number 2 the cell for incendiaries,* explaining that our sentence – three days without bread or water – would be either reduced or the opposite, according to our conduct. He shut the door on us, calmly pushed home the bolt, and told up to *appear before our judges on Thursday morning.* Heavens, how weak with rage I felt myself become; and Number Seven lost all his dignity on the spot, peeing all over the walls. For what else was there to do, I ask you, shut in that rat trap! Plunged into eternal night – *no lamps permitted to incendiaries* – (One little candle, sir? A match, Your Reverence?)

"Not even a match," he snapped back contemptuously. *"Murderers!"* That is how they treated us, those strangers!

Rotting there in the darkness, my head against the wall (which was the haunt of a thousand crawling things, of spiders whose feet I could feel tickling even inside my mouth), I reassured Number Seven by telling him that we were to have the good fortune of sleeping on the ground like early Christians, and of sharing the darkness of their Catacombs.

"But I wish I were somewhere else," said Number Seven. "I do wish I were somewhere else."

"But we shall get out of here, Fortuné. We shall get out. Anyway, at least we're not in prison. They can't put us in prison: you're too young, and I'm too sick. Don't be afraid, they're not going to hang us at dawn, as they did our great-grandfather Auguste! Grown-ups never put children in prison. It's not allowed. But where are we? I'd like to know that. An orphanage? It smells like an orphanage. A very nasty smell too, I must say. Perhaps we're in a hospital. Console yourself with the thought that all these things are possible. I'd rather we were in an orphanage, myself; I wouldn't like them to perform a major operation on me at dawn. But having considered the matter, I think we must be in an orphanage. You can go to sleep, Fortuné, there's nothing to be afraid of here. The Director is watching over us, and I am here, penknife in hand, to protect you. The darkness is a nuisance, I admit. But that's all we have to worry about, and we'll get used to it. We're lucky, Fortuné, everything is for the best. There is certainly an angel protecting us. I myself have about ten guardian angels, all hovering very kindly up there on the ceiling at this very moment. Sleep with a quiet mind, Fortuné. But Number Seven wouldn't go to sleep. He was afraid. And I myself, as I pressed my ear against the wall, could hear strange sighs and laments. Someone was being tortured, there could be no doubt of that. Perhaps the Director would give me a choice: your ears, your nose, or your little watch-ma-call-it. My left ear, please, sir, but cut it off quickly, I don't want it to hurt. But what about Number Seven? What will happen to Number Seven? (He was huddled against my shoulder now, wetting my cheek with his damp breath every time he exhaled.) What are you going to do with him, sir, he is young, very young, I ask you for pardon on his behalf, please, Your Grace.

"We are going to eat him for dessert, and keep his bones to play marbles with."

Oh, sir, don't do that! My grandmother has a weak heart, she would certainly have a stroke!

Worn out with my contemplation of the tortures that awaited us, I fell asleep. I woke again at frequent intervals to count the hours and scratch myself violently. I called upon all the saints in heaven to rescue us, but no one came. My dreams were peopled with clocks, and with the Scales of Good and Evil as Mlle Lorgnette and I had seen them depicted in the big illustrated catechism. Over the sound of my heart, I could hear Number Seven's beating like a pump. I was afraid, I was hungry, I was thirsty. Oh, St. Peter, St. Paul, and all you who look down upon my weakness. "Oh!" Number Seven said, "I wish I were somewhere else."

Two days passed in this way, there in the darkness, two days, three days spent rotting slowly away in that hole. Infuriated by our laments, the Director opened the door of our cell and threw a basinful of icy water on our faces, the water we needed to pull ourselves to our feet and stagger out into the corridor, where we were expected to stand in line with the others. It was dawn again, and cold. Number Seven rubbed his eyes as we walked into the Refectory. I remember there were bars across the windows, and I lowered my head so as not to see them.

I was unhappy. Every morning I woke up a little sadder than the evening before, my belly a little more racked with hunger. Holding my brother by the hand, I crept along close to the walls, afraid that one of the big tawny-haired killers who tore my blanket off my bed at night and stole my dry bread by day was going to plunge his dagger into the middle of my back. It wasn't an orphanage, it was a jungle. Dressed in rags, our greasy hair glued down over our eyes, we fought like wild animals as soon as the Director left us alone. Bloody feuds broke out everywhere, in the Refectory as well as on our only outing of the week, the Wednesday walk around the Institution grounds. But though we were all hardened fighters, the Director always knew how to find the chinks in our armour. Everyone trembled when he opened his mouth to speak. He spoke of Heavenly Justice, and of his duty to save the lost souls of the young. "Have no fear, my children," he said when he had finished thrashing us almost to death in front of a tribunal of Jesuits, who all kept their heads virtuously lowered over our files. "Have no fear, God's Mercy does exist, and we are keeping it in trust for you. We are not here to punish you, but to *rehabilitate you*." At night I imagined him coming into the dormitory, a hatchet in his hand, sniffing the smell of our piled-up bodies huddled against one another in pain and hunger. I imagined him severing, one by one, our lice-infested heads as they hung ready for the blow, tilting back into the void through the bars of the beds. During the day I never left my brother's side. Awful perils lay in wait for us wherever we turned: our neighbour at meals, threatening to put out our eyes with the prongs of his fork, or else, at night, a horde of perverts hunting us along the corridors to try to rape us. I wrote numerous letters to my grandmother, which the Director tore up as soon as they were written, smiling as he did so. He admired my style, he told me, but he thought it wrong of me to try to arouse sympathy for my misfortunes among grown-ups. He had himself written poems during his youth, he understood me, and he begged me to put my trust in him. He felt compassion for my weakness.

But remembering the times I had felt the blows of his fist on my jaw, I didn't put my trust in the Director. I put less and less trust in him as each day passed. Whenever the Wednesday walk came around, I attempted to escape, taking Number Seven with me, while the big boys with yellow hair were wallowing in the garbage, hoping to find a few scraps of food in the Director's trash can. On each occasion we were brought back to the Institution and severely punished for our insolence. It was not until a few days before Easter that Monsieur le Curé, sent by our grandmother with a basket of oranges and some clothes, and intending to stay only for the Sunday visiting hour, was so scandalized by our pale faces and our barbarous behaviour that he decided to take us with him, against the Director's orders. The tawny-haired seniors ate the oranges, and we ate the peel. That same evening we shared my grandmother's bed, and she woke us up several times during the night to cram us with delicious tidbits.

Several months later we were accused of theft, and consequently left home once more, this time for Our Lady of Mercy, a hotbed of delinquency no less luxuriant than the Reformatory. But being run by nuns, this new institution seemed to us to be lacking in severity.

Inspired by the example of the Director, Number Seven and I were determined to torture small children in our turn. We had many ideas for punishments and felt a great need to exercise our vengeance upon others weaker than ourselves. The nuns returned us into the safekeeping of Monsieur le Curé, as a precautionary measure. Happily, for we had fully intended to institute a general massacre of their other charges.

In the spring, Monsieur le Curé consecrated the new school, christening it The School of Repentance, and in the summer we stole in before vespers and made off with the three white candles lighting the dark little church. But in summer there were the woods to shelter us from our father's fury, and we were less afraid of the Reformatory. Number Seven spent his days up in the trees. He ate cherries and spat the pits down on my head. Lying stretched out in the grass, I let myself drink in the warmth of the sun. Number Seven only came down from his tree to take a dip in the spring and run back home for his bowl of soup. He occasionally read forbidden books over my shoulder, and dozed off beside me in the heat. The air was burning hot, and the sun was warm upon my chest, but I felt cold, as though I were still in the Reformatory. I was too tired even to move about on my cool, open-air bed, and it was through the mist of my fever that I watched Number Seven swinging from branch to branch and laughing. I was sick. I was afraid of dying. On the other hand, I knew that it wasn't possible for me to die, since death was reserved for babies and old people. I found reassurance in the thought that I was immortal, as I had been told so often by Monsieur le Curé and Grand-mère Antoinette. People don't die of flu. I was quite certain to get well again soon. Ah, the sky was clearing once more, I no longer coughed, I was breathing easily. *Immortal, remember that,* Monsieur le Curé had said, and I now realized that he was right. Number Seven jumped down from his tree. "Let's go for a swim!" I followed his example and took off my clothes. Life went on again. As in the days before the Reformatory, we sallied forth once more to chase the village girls and steal apples from Horace's orchard; then returned home on Friday evenings to receive our usual thrashing. But my grandmother put an end to my freedom and our excursions by keeping me more and more often in the house with her, pinned to her skirt, as it were. In the bitter fastness of my retreat I scribbled feverish poems that my grandmother threw into the fire as soon as her trembling, unlettered gaze fell upon such words as *passion* and *love* and *lust*. She would destroy the word *lust* on sight, but the word *honour* dissolved her in sighs of satisfaction.

"There is only one remedy," Monsieur le Curé said, his hands clasped over his ample belly, evidently irritated by my cough and by Number Seven's stifled giggles from the doorway. "There is always only one remedy . . . The Noviciat!"

"He'll leave tomorrow at daybreak," my grandmother said. "My mind is made up. Let's not speak of it again."

But in her clemency she waited until winter.

Well, I shall soon have reached the end of my story. The Noviciat is my tomb. There remains only for me to breathe my last, but I don't at all want to die. Yet Frère Théodule is being very good and helping me, and my confessor gives me advice. I recite the last prayers with him, but I still can't stop myself from thinking about other things, about running away. "Be quiet, my child, you must rest and close your eyes," Frère Théodule says, and I can feel the uneven flutter of my pulse under the moist pressure of his hand.

No, God, don't let me close my eyes, I don't want to, I don't want to!

"A little tea? A little beef broth?" Frère Théodule asks.

No, nothing. I've lost all my appetite. That's the saddest part, that I who was once so greedy – I've suddenly lost my appetite. In my dreams there is no longer anything hanging on the trees but rotten fruit, and I don't see flowers any more. It's winter everywhere. It's cold. But the saddest part, really, is to have lost my appetite.

Brother Théodule had gone to sleep, and the moonlight was streaming in on the dark patch his muddy boots were making on the bed. Jean Le Maigre got up. Someone was calling him from the doorway. Perhaps it was his grandmother bringing him clean clothes, or else Number Seven with a heavy basket in his arms, brimming with bunches of grapes and cherries. The grapes were overripe perhaps, and the cherries a touch too dark, but Jean Le Maigre was quite willing to eat them if they were offered. Jean Le Maigre began to dress, observing sadly that the hole in his pants had not yet been mended, or his socks darned. Perhaps Pomme would offer him some candy. And Alexis a new wool blanket. It might be his mother too, with her latest baby in her arms: Emmanuel, wrapped in his black swaddling clothes.

The timid voices were still calling to him. Jean, come and play with me. I'm lonely, Jean, come and warm me, Jean. Standing in the moonlight, he listened to them with a beating heart.

He would never reach the gate; it was too difficult to walk. He passed the bed where Brother Théodule was still snoring with half-open mouth. As he reached the dispensary, the smell of medicines made him stagger with sudden nausea, and he leaned against the wall, holding his breath. His heart was beating too hard. There was something moving about all the time in front of his eyes. He must not cough. Gently, he opened the door and felt the winter wind against his cheeks . . .

There they were, sitting on their bench in the recreation yard. Monsieur le Curé and his breviary, Grand-mère Antoinette concentrated on her rosary. And a little to one side, lit by the moonbeams,

Héloïse in ecstasy, her arms stretched out to form a cross, her dress open, baring her gently heaving white breasts. Farther off, he could see his mother weeping silently, her face in her hands. He felt sorry for her, but his attention was distracted by the voices, still calling to him from the skating rink.

"Jean, come and play with us, Jean!"

A greater surge of weakness swept through him once more as he tried to walk toward the gate. I'm coming, he called to his brothers. I'm running away! But his nose was bleeding again and he was afraid he wouldn't be able to make it. Monsieur le Curé lifted his eyes from his breviary.

"My poor child," he said, "you're going in the wrong direction again . . ."

But Jean Le Maigre had already opened the gate of the Noviciat. Just one more gate and he would be free. I shall be out on the road soon, he thought with satisfaction. Number Seven, Pomme, and Alexis were skating on the ice. They had no hats on and their scarves had come untied. Jean Le Maigre stood trembling dizzily at the edge of the frozen pond.

"Come on," said Number Seven, "we're going to teach you how."

But what a pity it is, Jean Le Maigre thought, what a pity it is I've lost my appetite. He looked down sadly at the golden blades of the skates that Number Seven and Pomme were helping him strap on.

"It'll be easier for you to run away with these on," said Number Seven as he put an arm around his brother's shoulders. "All you have to do now is follow us. We're going to skate all the way home. Let the wind carry you, and everything will be all right. But be careful you don't cough. Brother Théodule might hear us."

Jean Le Maigre skated off, surrounded by his brothers. It was so enjoyable, being able to skate without having had to learn. Jean

Le Maigre laughed aloud with pleasure. What a surprise! He was free at last! But suddenly it seemed as though the light in the sky had disappeared and his brothers had all abandoned him. He called to them, but they made no answer. He was alone again, and now he could see a long line of Jesuits coming across the crackling ice to judge him, their files tucked underneath their arms. He called out to his grandmother. She did not reply.

"There is nothing to be afraid of, my child," the Director said, walking toward him in his judge's robe. "We are not here to punish you but to bring you good news."

"Don't touch me," Jean Le Maigre answered, for the sight of the lustful smile on the Director's pallid face filled him with fear. "Oh, sir, let me run away! I'll never commit a sacrilege again, I promise I won't sir!"

The Director laid his hand on Jean Le Maigre's head.

"Calm yourself, my child," he said. "God's mercy is infinite. Look about you. Then you will understand."

Jean Le Maigre raised his uneasy gaze to the ring of Jesuits as they held up their files in a threatening wall around him.

"Oh, sir, let me be excused for a minute or two. I want to go out to the latrines."

"Not tonight," the Director answered. "Tonight you have been condemned to death. That's the good news we came to bring you. But if you don't cough, and if you don't cry, I promise you it won't hurt. Now turn around and lower your head."

Jean Le Maigre opened the neck of his shirt. He lowered his head. He had only to kneel down in the snow now and wait . . .

V

That same night, Héloïse lay pining on a strange bridal bed. She was languishing with desire beside her cruel Bridegroom, her hands clasped over her bosom, her wan gaze wandering across the ceiling. She had stripped herself of all her clothes in preparation for this rite; but inspired by some ceremonial sense of modesty, she had neglected to remove her black stockings, which were still held in place by two elastic bands that made scarlet circles around her long thin thighs. After all those hours of fasting and waiting, she was hungry, but her heart heaved with disgust at the thought of the now congealed meal that her grandmother had left outside her door the day before.

She was about to give herself once more, as she had in the past in the solitude of her cell, to the absent Beloved, who would leave within her those stigmata of love whose secret she would never divulge. But in the convent her Bridegroom's visits had been so sweet! She had greeted him without tears and without terror, yielding herself entirely to her tranquil torment, her terrible joy, eyes closed and body scarcely quivering beneath the thin white sheet that covered her.

Sometimes the Bridegroom's face would be imperceptibly transformed as it moved toward her. Misted over by her inner turmoil, it would assume tender and familiar features: the mouth of the young priest she had loved, the charming smile of Sister Saint Georges, who sat next to her in the Refectory, or the hollow, childish cheek of Mother Gabriel-des-Anges in charge of the Infirmary. Swathed in mysterious kisses, she bathed in the Bridegroom's embrace and tasted the greatest of all possible joys. But what humiliation when Mother Superior threw open her cell door with a cry of: "By heaven and all the fiends below! What's this I see in my convent?"

Héloïse sobbed in the chapel until dawn. Too bruised to pray, she felt the weakening murmurs of a too ephemeral pleasure fading on her lips.

The Bridegroom had changed. He could no longer take her and caress her as he had done before. He no longer rested upon her the beautiful and disturbing gaze that used at one time to precede her sacrifice. It was in the terror of his absence that Héloïse was giving herself to him now. She stretched out her hand in the bed. He wasn't there. He still hadn't come. He was late. Perhaps he wouldn't visit her at all that night.

She did not dare to move; she lay still, so as to feel the unexpected ravishment more acutely when it came. For now, as she was well aware, her body had been filled with too much suffering by her fasts, made too ugly by curious tortures, for her to feel herself truly a Bride. Touching that delicate wreck, kissing that bewildered brow, that fetid mouth, or moving down upon the utter purity of that cool neck was the work of a brutal ravisher. Was this the rape that Héloïse had dreamed of, during those chaste nights in the convent? "Let him take me, oh let him take me now, and I shall faint." But a few moments later she was struggling against the avenging Bridegroom as he bit her lips, then threw her back upon the bed as violently as he had taken her – and moaning quietly, she looked down at her abandoned breasts, gazed at her candid belly, and waited for the nocturnal wounds in her vanquished flesh to close again.

With fervent steps, Grand-mère Antoinette set out to pay a short early-morning visit to her dying charge. Preoccupied with First Communion in the neighbouring village, Monsieur le Curé had enjoined her to look after Horace in his stead. And it was with an air of triumph that Grand-mère Antoinette emerged from five o'clock Mass, radiant as a full moon beneath her impregnable armour of shawls, her bosom alert beneath the vast folds of her coat. She loved the clear dawns, the clean sky, the air like a sharp-ground knife, she was at home in the savage purity of the winter cold. But not in the snow, she had never liked the snow. "I don't hold it against you, God," she would grunt when a blizzard was blowing, out of breath from hauling her weary legs from one abyss of snow to the next. "I don't hold it against you, of course, but your church is really too far away." And Monsieur le Curé would throw her a disapproving glance, remarking severely, "Tch . . . tch . . . tch . . . Daughter, you must not blaspheme!" when she dared to express her annoyance under the church porch, gasping as she arrived: "Just as I thought, the Good Lord doesn't give a thought to my rheumatism! It's the same every day!"

When Number Seven and Pomme accompanied her, supposedly to serve as walking sticks or crutches, they would all find themselves shamefully sunk up to their knees in the snow, even before they reached the Cross at the crossroads. Grand-mère Antoinette therefore preferred to go to church alone, equipped like a foot soldier in her great rubber boots.

On days when it was fine she visited Horace, hoping that he would draw his last breath at some point during her visit. But despite his gangrene, the frequent attacks of paralysis in his right leg, and the mask of black pimples that covered his face, Horace was in good health. Grand-mère Antoinette fed him beef tea with a spoon and helped him to drink his pea soup. She also washed his shirt for him once a week; but since she lacked the patience to wait for it to dry by the fire, she always put it back on him again still wet.

"Aïe . . . Aïe . . . you'll be the death of me," Horace groaned, shaking his head to and fro on the pillow.

Grand-mère Antoinette only replied, "Don't complain, Horace, the Lord doesn't like to hear complaints!" And she darned the old man's socks, swept out the cabin, lit the stove, and brought in wood for the following day.

"Anchoinette, you're a good woman. Anchoinette, light my pipe for me!"

In moments when his pain grew excessive, Horace would spit out his false teeth, then brandish before a terrified Grand-mère Antoinette his green, naked gums with their threat of death.

To share the last joys of the dying man who had been put in her charge, Grand-mère Antoinette would take a puff or two at his pipe, talk to him about the weather, sigh when it was called for, reply to his echoing complaints with assenting nods, and round off all his comments with an *Oh you're so right,* delivered in tones of gravest melancholy. But not for an instant did she ever believe that the day would come for her to die as well; where her own death was concerned, she was blessedly tranquil. Had she not survived Grand-père Napoléon, even though he himself died at a very great age? Had she not survived her children and her grandchildren? Grand-père Napoléon still appeared to her sometimes in her sleep, a jealous ghost who threatened her with his raised fist.

"Napoléon, get on with your Purgatory and let me be," Grand-mère Antoinette would say to this phantom that haunted her nights. "Too many children, Napoléon, I gave you too many children."

Though Grand-mère Antoinette had yielded to her husband's demands, it was only in obedience to Monsieur le Curé, who in his sermons always spoke of *duty and a sense of duty,* and because it was the will of the Lord that she should have children. Grand-mère Antoinette still tasted the savour of a secret and bitter triumph when she remembered that her husband had never seen her body in the light of day. He had died without having known her, this man who had tried to conquer her with tenderness and terror, who had attempted in vain to storm the starched thickness of her petticoats, of her nightgowns, of the thousand and one subtle barriers she had invented to shelter herself from his caresses.

"Oh Lord, Horace, you look like him, you look like Napoléon this morning."

She had loved Napoléon on his deathbed. Treacherous and gentle, she was to be seen at his bedside, her cheeks flushed with zeal, an accomplice of approaching death, but full of solicitude for those last few moments of his life.

"Your hour is upon you, Horace, you ought to pray a little for your poor soul!"

"Ha ha!" Horace laughed through bubbles of saliva, "I got no wish to die, Anchoinette. Not today anyhow. Maybe tomorrow."

Horace disheartened Grand-mère Antoinette with his stubbornness. He too seemed to want to place on his brow an icy immortal crown. Raging inwardly, Grand-Mère Antoinette decided to let him live on for one more day.

"At your age, you should be ashamed of loving life so much, Horace!"

She got up from her chair complaining of her rheumatism; she washed Horace once more, without any feeling of disgust for that body already invaded by decay. She lifted him up tenderly from his bed, cradled him in her arms like a child, consoled him for his long suffering as though he were a newborn infant, and found herself thinking, with a sudden flood of nostalgia and distress rising in her heart, that the body resting on her knees was the light, perishable body of Jean Le Maigre . . .

It was thus that Grand-mère Antoinette decided, one cold winter morning after Mass, to pay a visit to the Noviciat. And so that she would not have to climb up into the train by herself, she took with her Pomme and Number Seven, torn from their uncertain slumbers, their cheeks white beneath their caps of hair, their trouser legs, by now too short, revealing pink circles of ankle chapped by the cold. For there was no railroad station, or if there was one, it provided no shelter from the wind. For Number Seven, that red cabin and its wooden bench had an atmosphere of ceremonial departure, and he compared them to the lonely open-air outhouses, and to his beloved exile out in the fields, where he had read so many travellers' tales, both by daylight and by the glow of a candle in the night.

Pomme, on the other hand, didn't even dare to open his eyes. Opening his eyes would have darkened the tranquil line of his horizon. In the train, he huddled down like a cat into his grandmother's woolly bosom. Yielding to the blank slumber empty of all cares, he scarcely felt the train as it jolted along at the edge of his dreams, but as the sun's warm caress touched his eyelids, he knew that the day was slowly rising and declining, keeping the same rhythm as his journey, and that he would soon open his eyes upon a motionless and golden evening. They arrived in the late afternoon, and Pomme, suddenly roused to wakefulness, glimpsed the dark shadow of the Noviciat in the distance, and then, crossing a rift torn open by the setting sun, a black bird in the sky.

Grand-mère Antoinette walked behind Brother Théodule into the infirmary, breathing in an unmistakable odour as she followed in his wake: the smell of death. In the empty dormitory, so disturbingly white as to make the spectator dizzy, Grand-mère Antoinette noticed that they had stripped Jean Le Maigre's bed, emptied his locker, and arranged his manuscripts on the table. She could also see the dried-up ink in the bottom of the inkwell, and the marks of his short, impatient teeth on the half-chewed pencils. Opening the slim exercise books one by one, she saw the letters Jean Le Maigre had formed with such concentration, with such concentration and with such despair; for certain words had lost some of their syllables where a sudden languor had stayed his hand in the middle of a sentence or a paragraph. Each exercise book revealed a different phase in the progress of Jean Le Maigre's illness, a sad and joyful ardour constantly on the brink of a final fatigue. Grand-mère Antoinette would have liked to clutch these pages to her breast, to imprint each one forever in her heart while its pain and its savage secret were still fresh. But she was overwhelmed with shame and unable to make any gesture while Brother Théodule was there. In any case, she had other things to worry about than weeping for a dead grandchild! Since she had arrived just in time for Jean Le Maigre's funeral, she had to think about paying for a tombstone. "Ah, all these deaths are ruining me!" she thought with a shrug of the shoulders. "And this one even more than all the others!"

"He must have a beautiful grave," Grand-mère Antoinette said after a moment's silence. "I want Jean Le Maigre to be proud of me, right to the end. Yes, a beautiful funeral," she went on, with candour and humility, "a lot of Masses said for his soul, a lot of flowers. He was so fond of ceremonies!"

But Grand-mère Antoinette's heart shrank within her once more as she scratched away the frost on the window with her nail, for there outside was the cemetery beneath the trees, the green reflection of the moon across the snow . . .

Kneeling beside their grandmother in the Noviciat chapel, Pomme and Number Seven rubbed their eyes already reddened by emotion. They had never known any music but the quavering hymns sung by the Children of Mary in their own parish, or the frail lament from their own church organ, and were filled with wonder by the Choir of Novices, whose voices streamed forth untamed from the depths of childhood – and sometimes, too, so delicately that they seemed about to shiver like crystal against the walls. So the words of the *Libera me, Domine, de morte aeterna* rang out in tones of joy on this day that Jean Le Maigre, in his imagination, had clothed with a dark, funereal aura. The novices hurled themselves with even greater abandon into the *Kyrie eleison*, and even Grand-mère Antoinette could not suppress a quiver of hope as she listened to them. After all, she thought, it's not all as sad as I think it is. Jean Le Maigre won't be as cold in heaven as he was on earth. He won't have an earache any more, and he did suffer so much down here, poor child – quickly, O Lord! have mercy on him!

She was proud of her tears and shed a great many as she prayed. I want him to be in heaven, Lord, I want him to be in heaven. (The novices ended the *Ite, missa est* on a note of such strident plangency that Grand-mère Antoinette was forced to drive away the fragile spectre of Jean Le Maigre delivered over to the flames of Purgatory.) Her tears having at last succeeded in putting out the red-hot coals of hell, Grand-mère Antoinette was forced to blow her nose with considerable violence as she passed from the Mass to the burial itself, as though from one spectacle of suffering to the next. It was not until Jean Le Maigre's coffin slid down into the earth, disappearing slowly into its pit of muddy earth and snow beneath the Young Brothers' offerings (each of them ceremoniously cast a white flower in turn upon the grave of the dead boy, later to bear the name of BROTHER JOHN JOACHIM AMBROSE OF THE SORROWS, with the air of people to whom burials were an everyday occurrence, the same air of communal indifference with which they had sung the *Requiem* a few minutes earlier, in the chapel), that Number Seven and his brother began to be aware of the gravity of the event. But they were distracted by the sound of the bells, by the sudden rustling of a flight of crows among the cemetery trees, so that from time to time they could not help forgetting the brother whose loss they were mourning with such ardour. *Ra-ora-pro-nobis*, the Little Brothers chanted in chorus, one hand clutching their cassocks as they flapped in the wind, while the stronger voices of the priests drowned their murmurs with a PRO-NO-BIS declaimed in heavier and more lugubrious tones.

All the same, Grand-mère Antoinette thought, filled with pride at her decision to have her grandson buried on a hillside, and scattering on his grave a generous handful of the grain she always kept stored away in her pockets for the birds – all the same, he'll be better off here than at home. Too much wind, possibly, but he'll get used to it . . .

Requiem aeternam dona ei, Domine murmured the choir, and lifting her eyes up to the sky, Grand-mère Antoinette felt the air turn colder against her cheeks and saw that the clouds were darker now on the horizon.

Pomme and Number Seven took off their black felt hats, and standing beside their grandmother, they made the sign of the cross.

Héloïse was getting ready to leave. Sitting on the edge of her bed in her nun's robe, her delicate and languid features turned toward the window, she was slowly coming back to life. The sunbeams falling on the grey walls of her room seemed to light up the disorder in which the young woman had been living for the past few months, as though in the company of a painful and exhausted madness. This disorder consisted of no more than a few objects abandoned in one corner, some food wrapped up in a piece of yellowing paper, a bloodstained sheet violently thrust away under the bed in a moment of shame, an open suitcase, and, lying on the dirty floor, a crucifix and some letters, whole piles of letters that Héloïse had never had the courage to send to the people they were written to, which she was now reading silently to herself in the solitude of her room. She did not hear the cries of the baby from the kitchen. Surrounded by those muted laments to which she was now accustomed, like a deaf woman in the buzzing of her own silence, she saw again the curious dream she had had that night.

She was pushing open the gate of the convent again, escorted by Sister George of the Wrath, who gave her back the key of her cell with a recommendation not to let her confessor visit her at night, and not to say her prayers aloud, lest she wake up the Mother Superior. Héloïse humbly bowed her head as she answered, "Yes, Sister, yes, Mother," in a childlike voice. In the chapel, instead of chanting vespers, each with a candle in her hand, as was usual on Easter Day, the novices filled the holy place with laughing cries, with surprised applause; and one by one, their coifs thrown nonchalantly back on their shoulders as they passed in front of Héloïse, performing a delighted dance, they loosened their long tresses, brown or blond, that the coifs had held so long imprisoned in the black tissue of their threads.

Héloïse herself was forced to uncover her head before joining her companions, and it was with the same sweet sensations of sacrilege that she felt her hair float freely around her neck, then unroll deliciously upon her shoulders in warm curls the colour of ripe corn. Her confessor interrupted this gush of well-being by thrusting the nuns harshly aside on his way to the altar, and saying:

"It is now the turn of *Sister Héloïse of the Martyrs and of the Blood Shed for Christ* to make public confession . . . I have with me here all the documents leading to her conviction. The Reverend Mother Superior has put all the letters Sister Héloïse has written into my hands. Let the good Sister Héloïse consent to have her hair shorn off in peace and I will then give her my blessing."

With that terrible humility that always threatens even the most heedless and proud of dreamers, that surrounds the most beautiful of dreams and the most innocent of trances with a shadow of vague shame, with an indefinable uneasiness, Héloïse sat there beside her companions as they choked back their laughter on the long lines of benches, and gently wept. It seemed to her that they had all betrayed her, that her confessor himself, who at that moment was reading out to all those nuns, suddenly transformed into spiteful and frivolous young women, those absurdly secret letters that Héloïse had written to some of her companions, begging for their help or for some measure of austere affection; it seemed to her that he too, this man whom she had loved, had loved in the same daring and tender secrecy, was taking pleasure in humiliating her, like the others. Was he not laughing at her cruelly? Was he not imitating the voice of her distress as he read out to Sister George of the Wrath in mock-loving tones:

> *Oh Sister George of the Wrath, in your*
> *Celestial embrace*
> *I swoon and die . . .*

and to Sister Philomène of the Patience, who was blushing with pride, these fevered words:

> *Well-beloved Sister Philomène, you in whose*
> *heart mercy forever springs,'*
> *absolve my passion . . .*

He, too, had the power of torturing her, of inspiring her with a limitless shame . . . Héloïse wept and wept, finding no shoulder to comfort her, she who had been so happy a few moments before, dancing in the sunlit chapel. (Her sobs did not awaken the Mother Superior, who was huddled against the wall in a heavy sleep, her face sunk in her bosom.) Héloïse's soul had been laid bare, and not only her soul but her body as well. (Had they not cut off her hair in front of everyone, and shaved her head? She touched the stubble on her neck, the naked skin on her scalp . . .) And her most silent passions, her most hidden loves had denied her publicly in the most degrading manner. Little by little, the day moved to its close, the light faded from the stained-glass windows in the chapel, and Héloïse could breathe again.

Safely cradled in her everyday misery, and suddenly filled with gratitude, she opened her eyes and looked around at the grey walls of her room once more . . .

The men had left the house before daybreak, forgetting their bowls of coffee growing cold on the table and their dirty plates piled on the stove. They must have eaten standing up, their eyes fixed on the window, impatient and anxious at the thought of the day's work ahead. Héloïse had scrubbed herself violently, and the cold water had done her good. Sitting by the child's cradle, her idle hands upon her knees, she lingered before leaving, her suitcase on the floor beside her. She was enveloped in a topcoat that was too long for her and allowed nothing to show but the two black lines of her thick stockings. Shoulders sagging, eyes vaguely oppressed, she might have been her mother, even if only for a moment, as she turned to the child and cradled him in her arms before taking off his wet clothes. Suddenly she seemed to have in common with her mother a rough tenderness bordering on disgust.

Now Emmanuel was asleep. Héloïse was thinking of something else. She felt desire welling up in her breast once again – and closing her eyes, she gave herself up to the sad dream of love that she had dreamed that night. This time the convent had been transformed into a joyful tavern frequented by fat, bearded men, and by young men with pink cheeks, to whom Héloïse had offered hospitality for the night. She received them in her cell. The other nuns were burning incense in the kitchen for their visitors. Héloïse was loved.

The men didn't seem to notice her wasted body, or the sweat of fatigue that dampened all her clothes with a long, dark stain. The young men eyed her covetously, and she offered herself humbly to the boldest of caresses, to furious embraces that left her trembling with fright and pleasure on her bed. Héloïse, Héloïse, the Mother

Superior suddenly cried, wrenching open the door of her cell, *you have lost your soul my poor child!*

That was how it always ended, this dream that Héloïse had dreamed so many times in her solitary nights. She was never to dream that dream again. It was to become her real domain, the compass of her life.

By ten o'clock, Héloïse had left the house. She left regretting that she would not hear her sisters' voices as they came back from the farm, quarrelling on the stairs, their thick, boys' voices, their heavy tread; that day, for the first time, she would have been glad to hear them . . .

VI

Winter was drawing to a close. Grand-mère Antoinette was growing wan with solitude in her armchair. Héloïse would not be coming down any more for evening prayers. The men only came back to eat and sleep. Grand-mère Antoinette was bored. Her eyes were aloof as they passed without lingering over her daughter sitting at the table, or one of the younger boys dozing in a corner with his arms around an emaciated dog, its muzzle stretched along the floor toward the warmth emanating from the stove. Anita, Roberta, Aurelia no longer dared come near Grand-mère Antoinette since Jean Le Maigre's death. They disappeared up into their room before it was time for evening prayers. Huddled against each other in the dark, they talked in whispers, choking back coarse, muffled exclamations. Grand-mère Antoinette flew into a temper at the slightest noise, she who in the past had been surprised on so many occasions by the imperious reverberations of her own voice. She spoke less and less – hardly at all in the end, except to express her anger and crush her son-in-law. She accused him openly of having killed Jean Le Maigre with negligence, with his idleness. She scolded him too, though with more composure, for his inability to read, even though she herself found it a wretched struggle to decipher Jean Le Maigre's writing as she continued her self-appointed task of reading all his manuscripts to the very last line. (She carried them around with her everywhere, lest some heartless hand should throw them into the fire.) The father never allowed himself to be disturbed by her reproaches. Since he could not afford to feed two laggards who did nothing but wander through the village stealing the neighbours' chickens instead of going to school, he had taken Pomme and Number Seven into town and found them work as apprentices in a boot factory. The brothers had been delighted with their father's decision and had said goodbye to their grandmother with the utmost serenity, joy on their faces, eyes misty with gratitude that they would be able to earn a wage at last . . .

"Oh heavens," Grand-mère Antoinette said, "have pity on those two creatures being led to slaughter . . ."

Wallowing in the vomit with which he had filled his cradle, his little eyes glittering beneath their wrinkled lids, Emmanuel had been in the best of health ever since Jean Le Maigre had died. To console herself for the loss of her son, having doubtless discovered that Jean Le Maigre, like several of her other children, was dearer to her dead than he had ever been alive, the mother had now turned her attentions toward Emmanuel and was nervously weaning him from her withered breasts. Grand-mère Antoinette, on the other hand, looked down upon Emmanuel from the heights of her constant ill humour, and had already taken to scolding him for all the defects that she condemned so severely in his father. All of which did not prevent Emmanuel from provoking his grandmother with piercing, parrot-like cries and the daily tide that flowed out from his leaky cradle and trickled across the floor. And when there was no one else in the house, during the afternoon, the baby and the old woman did in fact seem to converse with each other in their own way, gently at first, as birds do, then suddenly filling the air with threats and challenges, each displaying contentedly to the other the war-like spirit that they both possessed.

But the days passed, and Grand-mère Antoinette would allow no one to come and sit beside her armchair, as Jean Le Maigre had so often done, curling up his long legs and stretching his neck to watch his grandmother as she sat knitting or doing her embroidery. New seasons would come and go, Emmanuel would grow up into a little boy, and he too perhaps – who knows? – would one day have a special place reserved for him in the old woman's heart. But she was too proud of the pain she cherished in her heart to want to seek a cure for it. Jean Le Maigre was still too much alive to her, for she was reading the works he had left behind – allowing herself, like Monsieur le Curé, though even more ignorantly, to condemn the author for his blasphemies, and exclaiming lovingly on every page, *How shocking oh Lord how shocking*, Monsieur le Curé is right, these exercise books must be torn up right away! And yet she postponed the act, and turning the pages with impatience, she continued her journey further and further back, toward the reality of her grandson's life, losing her temper with a word that would not bow to her intelligence, with a symbol that would not yield its secret, until she became jealous even of those yellowed pages, because Jean Le Maigre had given more of himself to them than he ever had to her. Sometimes she even lost her temper with Jean Le Maigre himself when, refined and lewd by turns, he wrote in his *Family Prophecies* that his brother Pomme would end up in prison, Number Seven on the scaffold, and Héloïse his sister in a brothel. (Pausing at the line, "A sequestered country tavern," Grand-mère Antoinette failed to grasp its import.) Jean Le Maigre had also written that his grandmother would die of immortality at an advanced age and that his brother Emmanuel *now weeping the bitter tears of the newly born* would end up in the Noviciat and succumb to the same honourable disease that Jean Le Maigre had suffered from himself.

"Horrors! Oh, horrors!" Grand-mère Antoinette exclaimed, but still she continued to fortify her love, to feed her pride with the confidences her grandson Jean Le Maigre, that soul whose courage had not quailed even at blasphemy, had left behind.

Before her, then, there passed the curious silhouettes of Marthe-the-Little-Hunchback (and of Marguerite-with-the-Long-Legs as well, and Jocelyne whose hair was full of lice, and

> *Beloved Carmen of the rose and the tulips*
> *Who brought me bonbons at Easter . . .*

of Brother Théodule, who prowled at night through the junior dormitory, of the Director, of . . . in short, all those shades that had haunted the more or less chaste nights of Jean Le Maigre with *the sweet torture of the senses*. But Grand-mère Antoinette knew how to be discreet, how to close her eyes, how to console herself with the thought that all these creatures (thanks be to God) were nothing but figments of the imagination and could never have existed in reality.

Passing from *the shadowy caress upon my brow*, Jean Le Maigre had finished his life surrounded by violence and crime:

> *They will kill him oh Lord they will kill him*
> *In the white sky above I see*
> *Their avenging knife*
> *I can hear the savage cries*
> *Interrupted by my Requiem . . .*

"A bad end, a very bad end," Grand-mère Antoinette thought to herself, "truly a very sad death." But in fact she believed nothing of the kind. Jean Le Maigre had never appeared so virtuous in her eyes as he had since his death, or in such good health as he did now, laid in his grave, "very quiet, up there, on the hillside . . ." And yet it seemed to her, too, that the winter was longer than usual, that the days lasted too long, that the nights were not as restful as they had been. It must be that she was starting to grow old. It was certain she had aged a great deal, even in the past few days . . .

Jean Le Maigre's lack of caution in scattering poems, letters, or sections of his private diary wherever he went had provided a fruitful harvest for Brother Théodule's curiosity. And Brother Théodule was now enjoying these fruits, with humid eye and trembling lips. As his delicate white fingers, in imagination touching Jean Le Maigre's warm corpse, brushed their tips over the rough-textured paper, following the lines of childish letters, so the G's, the L's, the C's, and all the others with fresh and rounded curves evoked in the poor Brother other forms that he had known, sensations of past intimacy. (Though for the ordinary reader they were no more than clumsy blots of ink soiling Jean Le Maigre's finest poetic flights with their crude smudges.) Whereas the A's, the V's, and the U's all quivered like cheeks caressed by a warm autumnal breeze . . . Just as Brother Théodule had possessed Narcisse, Brother Paul, and Brother Victor. (He was very young, Brother Victor, the Father Superior had observed, they die very young in your infirmary! Brother Théodule had humbly bowed his head. "Man prays, God decides. I did my duty.") And Narcisse had this inscription upon his grave:

BROTHER NARCISSE DIED AGED 12 years 6 months
To the angels   paradise
To the innocent   eternity
Amen

And Paul, that magnificent child!

BROTHER PAUL OF THE CROSS
13 years one month
May you be crowned with light
beloved mortal

As he had ravished their souls, so Brother Théodule now possessed Jean Le Maigre. Unlike those who had preceded him to a similar fate, Jean Le Maigre had had no need of beauty to seduce the Devil. In fact, it was his charming homeliness itself that had ensured the victory – or rather, Brother Théodule had been moved by something indefinably mysterious and touching in Jean Le Maigre. His exquisite madness perhaps, or something even more disturbing: the inherent aptitude the young boy had for what Brother Théodule always referred to as *evil*, though without seeking to define it. At all events, Brother Théodule had never had a disciple so quick to follow him, or a prey so lighthearted and gay in the midst of peril. Without knowing it, Jean Le Maigre had brought the Devil a short but refreshing respite from his obsessions and had left behind him (for a few days, at least) the memory of a rapturous comradeship, and one still shot through with tenderness. But it was rather late to start thinking of deliverance. The Brother Superior had already fixed a suspicious eye upon his Nursing Brother.

"And Brother Narcisse, what exactly did he die of?"

"Of scarlet fever, Brother Superior, like so many others. Ah, the Lord is very hard!"

But Brother Théodule was forced to admit later that he had quenched his patient's fever by plunging him into an ice-cold bath. From this clumsy confession he went on to another. Brother Jean had fallen into his everlasting sleep (a mistake, a simple mistake, Brother) amid clouds of ether, during one of the singular experiments that Brother Théodule was wont to conduct in his laboratory. And then Brother Frédérick . . .

"Stop! I don't wish to hear another word!" the Superior cried in alarm. "You must leave this Noviciat tonight at the very latest!"

Disappointed that he had not gained the attention of the bishops and the cardinals, who thronged his imagination during the melancholy hours he spent chasing little boys along the Noviciat's evil-smelling corridors, Brother Théodule left as sadly as he had come, wearing his thick, dirty boots, clothed in his pauper's rags, looking exactly as he had looked at the time of his precocious entry into the Noviciat a few years before. Alas, he thought, God had deceived him . . . He had believed, like so many of his fellows in misfortune, that God would grant him not only forgiveness for his faults to come, whose burning weight he could already feel, but also the calm security that vices need if they are to flourish, and then, like plants, to flower in the light of day.

Brother Théodule had not lost any time since Jean Le Maigre's death. He had already selected other Jeans to suit his purposes, two or three boys with curly hair and dreamy voices, whom the Superior expelled at the same time as the Devil, reminding them that in hell *you will burn where you sinned,* and accompanying these words with shameful punishments they would remember all their lives, these criminals with angels' faces who had served their apprenticeship to vice within the walls of orphanages and convents, and who asked nothing better than to exchange that wild Eden of their idle senses for liberty at last.

Brother Théodule knotted his bootlaces and sniffed back his tears. He was still young, and alone in the world . . . (No mother, no home, and a ruined vocation, he would never eat at set hours again, never sleep in clean sheets, never be able to use soap when he washed, and now that his salvation was in doubt, God would no longer shield him from temptation. Ah, how was it possible that he could be so unhappy?) He was going back to the whistles, to the signals in shadowy churches or at the gates of schools as the students were let out, back to his anxious pursuit along the beaches, along the banks of streams where children played their indecent games for him to watch unseen – his chin buried in the collar of his coat, smoking, smoking ceaselessly, a crumpled cigarette between his trembling fingers. ("Forgive me, Father, I won't do it any more, I promise, Father." "Go in peace, my son, and sin no more.") He went in peace, then began doing it again next day, or, given the chance, the very same day as his confession. But he was still filled with a great hope as he felt that God was waiting for him in every church, that he would go on receiving His forgiveness like a special food containing the precious energy he needed to accomplish evil – the moment he had received its benison . . .

"Lord, oh Lord, have pity on my lost dignity!"

But with what ardour he continue to stalk the delight of prayer, with what impulsive faith he hurled himself upon his adolescent victims, then murmured in their ears those same weak words of adoration and despair that he used also when addressing God in supplication.

Never having known the sweetness of a mother's breast, he had been the enemy of all women and all mothers since his birth. He had grown up in the midst of priests, in the sombre forest of the Brothers, driven from one Noviciat to the next, but taking a boastful pride in the bad image they had of him.

"But what does it matter, oh Lord," he thought as he laced up his boots, "what does it matter. I am free, I am going into the world . . ." In his mind was the thought that women would draw aside henceforth as he passed, that mothers would look at him with stern eyes. (And who knows, perhaps draw away from him with that movement of distaste that froze his heart?) "That man has chosen our sons to prey upon . . ." he would feel them thinking as he passed by them in the street. "That man is accursed for his impure deeds."

"But," he also thought, "everything will be all right, I shall give lessons, I shall teach the piano . . . I shall have a room of my own, I shall buy books for myself, and begin again, begin all over again, yes, that's it, I shall give private lessons . . ."

He stood up, buttoned his shirt, smoked a cigarette as he walked for the last time around his infirmary, without a glance at the bed where Jean Le Maigre had died (he had relinquished life so peacefully that Brother Théodule had not even noticed it; a few minutes before, he had asked for the exact time, then for a little tea – a lot of sugar in it, please – simple, entirely unprophetic words that Brother Théodule had scarcely heard . . .), where he had closed his eyes, without the last rites, with the utmost docility, as though the act of dying had really been of no concern to him (or so Brother Théodule believed at least). With lowered head, eyes fixed on the toes of his big boots, Brother Théodule thought that he was nothing but a young, uncultured man, that everything about him (down to the badly pressed creases in his trousers) had the same ineluctable look of commonness and failure. But despite this shabby outward appearance of poverty and misfortune, he was still formidable, he thought, he could still make himself feared.

(Yes, they will write about me in the newspapers, everyone will know, I shall make them afraid to the very end, I shall take their sons, I shall take them out and hang them on trees, I shall strangle them . . . I . . .) He wiped away the sweat that was trickling down his forehead. Swiftly, he sought help from God. Collecting his mind for a short while, between clasped hands, he experience a few moments of peace.

In the afternoon, Grand-mère would sit and talk to Emmanuel as she knitted interminable multicoloured socks – green, blue, red, striped, and then, as the hours went by, tinged with the added colours of the setting sun. Bouncing with joy, Emmanuel clapped his hands and feet together and brimmed over with such good humour and curiosity that Grand-mère Antoinette was in a constant state of alarm lest he jump right out of his cradle. (So curious was he, in fact, that his grandmother was obliged several times to unclench his fingers from her knitting needles, or from the pins pinned on her bodice, which he seized and attempted to eat whenever she leaned over to take a closer look at him . . .)

"Ah!" she said, "you're just like him, you're full of curiosity, just like Jean Le Maigre."

This remark filled Emmanuel with a legitimate pride that made his cries louder and even more high-pitched. From Emmanuel's point of view, the landscape represented by Grand-mère Antoinette was growing daily in extent. His grandmother's nose had the majesty of a swelling hill, her cheeks the whiteness of snow, and from her mouth there blew a breath as cold as winter winds. And Grand-mère Antoinette's ears! To Emmanuel they were objects of delight and love! You could bite into them like cherries; and sometimes you could even play with grandmother's nose, when she allowed it, in moments of distraction.

"Rascal, little rascal," the old woman said, scolding but gentle, pushing him away and drawing him to her at the same time, as though he were a little bear cub she wanted to tumble on the floor with her own great paws, partly to amuse him and partly to teach him obedience.

As a revenge for the gloomy indifference with which his mother had suckled him during the first few days of his life, Emmanuel would sometimes behave as though she did not exist, pretending to prefer the rough caresses of his grandmother. But in the evening, she had only to walk over to him and he would immediately search out her breast and fasten his thirsty lips upon it. And then his mother would enfold him in the silent sheltering wing of sleep.

At night he slept in the same bedroom as his parents, cut off from his mother by his father's long shadow, which filled up all his dreams, whether of the present or of the future, with sacred terror. Several times, as he grew older, he was to see that brutal silhouette moving to and fro in the room. (Was he not the intruder, the giant enemy who raped his mother every night, as she lay moaning in a gentle whisper, "Please, the children are listening . . ." But suddenly he would silence her, and Emmanuel could no longer hear anything but delicate sighs and stifled murmurs. "No . . . No, oh Lord, no!" or else the "I'm . . . too . . . tired . . ." that brought their uninterrupted embrace to an abrupt end.)

Motionless in his bed, fists clenched, he would continue to listen until exhaustion put an end to those supplications of joy and suffering, ashamed that his mother should have to obey this man who gave her orders in the night. Their ears pressed to the dividing wall, Anita, Roberta, and Aurelia were also listening to this nocturnal tumult in their parents' room. But they revelled in it as though it were some savage celebration that would release the budding shamelessness they sensed inside themselves. (For what did they know of life, these young girls, who, as spring drew near, looked more and more like languid nanny goats caught in the thickets of their hair – what did they know of men, except for the lovesick youths who came timidly to the house on Sundays to ask for their hands in marriage, boys with naked feet inside heavy shoes, still dressed in their everyday blue coveralls with the apron fronts, and their white cotton shirts with open necks? Chaperoned by the Elder Brothers, who kept watch from behind their newspapers, screened by the blue curtain rising from their line of pipes, what had the girls to hope for from these pimply young men who came to call, then did not even dare to look at them?)

But dawn came quickly, and a first red flame was soon caressing the white frost on the windowpanes, though without burning off the patterns it had made; the light of day came piercing into the room, and at last Emmanuel heard the five chimes from the clock . . . *Ding Dong Ding Dong Dong,* heralding his grandmother's footsteps in the passage, the *Co-ca-ri-co* of the cock in the yard, swiftly followed by the appearance of his grandmother in the doorway, evoking the *Co-ca-rico* of the cock once more with the black and white crest of hair that sprang up bristling from her forehead.

What a haven Grand-mère Antoinette's bedroom was for the younger boys as they lay huddled there in a disordered, slumbering heap, together with the dog and cat (and occasionally a sheep that Grand-mère Antoinette had rescued from the cold night outside), the former with their red legs lolling out here and there through the bars of the bed, the latter with their paws calmly laid out along the warm floorboards, seemingly lost in a careless, incorruptible sleep, but betraying even in their slumbers, by the slightest quiver of a tail, by the tiniest twitch of an ear, the restless curiosity of their nature. Here, Emmanuel and Grand-mère Antoinette could continue their conversation of the day before. Grand-mère Antoinette talked a great deal at dawn. Emmanuel nestled himself against her, trying to steal a little warmth.

"Let's see," she would say, "what was it I was saying? Oh you, of course you never listen, all you think about is yourself . . ." Emmanuel was no longer cold, but he was beginning to feel hungry. It was always the same when his grandmother started telling him a story. He would suddenly remember that he was hungry, terribly hungry. Performing a habitual caress, Grand-mère Antoinette picked up both Emmanuel's feet together in one hand, like two eggs in a single nest, and told him to be good, "and not to wriggle about like a little worm."

Then Grand-mère Antoinette told him of her misfortunes. "Bad news, Emmanuel, we've had very bad news, I don't know what's to become of us."

But he was very fond of bad news, as a matter of fact. Like his brothers, he was to love gales and hurricanes, shipwrecks and funerals, when he grew up. Would she tell him about Héloïse today, or about Pomme, who had just cut off three fingers of his left hand in the factory, or about Number Seven and how Uncle Armandin Laframboise was ill-treating him now that Number Seven was staying with him in the town?

"Things are going badly for us, Emmanuel, very badly . . ."

Though she also said that everything was going very well, since Number Seven still sent his wages home every week, and Pomme was safe in the hospital, and Héloïse was miraculously earning a great deal of money – at the PUBLIC ROSE TAVERN – and her dear good neighbour Horace was feeling better in spite of the pus that puffed up his cheeks and the shadowy veil that was slowly falling over his eyes . . .

"Yes, everything could be a lot worse . . .

"Perhaps they'll sew his fingers back on in the hospital, who knows? It will teach him not to go poking his hands in anywhere he pleases, trying to steal! And Horace has coped with much worse than this, he'll pull out of it, blind or not – after all, that won't stop him from breathing! And Héloïse too, it'll do her good to meet a lot of new people, when you think how she never used to leave her bedroom . . . Do you know your Uncle Armandin Laframboise? He has twelve boys, twelve devils. Thrashes them all once a day. They were all well brought up. But unfortunately, no education! So what's the point in going to live in the town, eh? There's not one of them with the slightest intelligence. Not like here. Léopold now, he was as cunning as a fox, and Jean Le Maigre too, so clever it was frightening! If you could have seen him writing his Latin poems on my knee, so intelligent that he made be blush with his questions! He wanted to know everything, poor child. It was his curiosity that killed him. His father beat him too much. You'll be beaten, too, if you ask questions. Better to keep quiet and go out to chop wood like the others. Yes, that's the best way. Héloïse was talented too, Monsieur le Curé always said. I don't know what she did with her gifts, though. She could embroider when she was six (unfortunately, we had no thread in the house), and the lady schoolteacher said she had a gift for drawing. She used to draw all day on the blackboard at school. But your Uncle Armandin Laframboise's twelve boys (fourteen, with Number Seven and Pomme, who are living with him at the moment) are barbarians, they don't know how to do anything! At twelve, school, higher education, everything thrown out the window. Think of it! Every morning they all leave home to go to the factory, to the plant, to the bakery – and I don't know what else . . . They're little still, and there they are, getting their fingers cut off in a boot factory or poisoning their lungs in a tobacco factory. Oh Lord, forgive us our trespasses! I've told your father, I've tried to make him understand –

"Pomme is only eleven, he's too young to go to work in the town. I want to keep him here with me. He can make himself useful to me. He can go and help Monsieur le Curé in the vestry on Saturdays . . .

"But your father is as stubborn as an ox, as simple as a fish! He throws his children out of the house before they know how to fend for themselves like grown-up men. I wonder what will become of him without those three fingers. Apparently he's quite thin now, and they don't feed him properly at the hospital. Your Uncle Armandin Laframboise wrote to tell me all about it, without so much as a single sigh! A man without a heart – just like your father. And one who can't spell, what's more:

> In hospital the littlest of the two
> Put his fingers in the mache machine
> Didn't lose his hand
> Only three fingers
> Armandin Laframboise
> *Wishes for yur good helth*
> *For the New Year*

"In what machine? One can't help wondering. Something sharp, that's for sure. And Number Seven too, he thinks about nothing but his calves and his cows and his pigs, though he would not so much as set foot in the cowsheds when he was here."

> And the cow Clementine, grandma
> And the little calf grandma
> With markings or without markings

And the pig Marthuroulou
What colour is it
Grandma

"Don't know a single one of those animals," Grand-mère Antoinette commented to Emmanuel. "There isn't time to christen every creature that's born. But I don't like this business of the fingers in the machine, I don't like that at all! To begin with, what did those people in the hospital do with the fingers?" (At which point she glimpsed the hand lying on a silver charger, like John the Baptist's head, exiled forever from Pomme's body, round and calm, as fresh as a pear put out to ripen in the sun.) "And Uncle Armandin Laframboise has written to say they made him wait two hours at the hospital before attending to him."

As I had no money
He was bleeding as we waited
My wife came with the money
They put him on an operating table
We have not seen him
                    since
As I have always told you Antoinette
money is necessary
For the important happenings in life
                    accidents
                    and funerals
It's very necessary
Perhaps it wasn't an operating table
Anyway it was a table
So leave your farm Antoinette
And those fields of yours that don't give any crops
Come and live here Antoinette

My wife had been pregnant since June
We are just two steps from the factory
The trains go right by the house
Lots of smoke Antoinette
So come and live with us!

"But now," Emmanuel thought as he dozed against his grandmother's chest, "I am beginning to be hungry."

"And Héloïse, she doesn't go to Mass any more. She writes that she doesn't have the time. She says there's a telephone in the tavern, and electricity. Oh, it's very different from here. Life abroad is not to be sneezed at, of course, Emmanuel – but in spite of everything, we're very comfortable here, in the evening, with our oil lamp. Your father doesn't want electricity put in, and he's right. I'm against progress too. But what about you, Emmanuel, what do you think about it, eh?"

She got up at last. At the rustling of her nightgown, at the sound of her steps on the stairs, the younger boys gently awoke, bare-legged, in a confusion of dishevelled hair and outstretched arms, and with them the cat and the dog, suddenly impatient to run outside, tail wagging, ears pricked, opening wide eyes still drowned in the waxy mists of sleep.

VII

Héloïse kept up a regular correspondence with the merchants who lived in the town, with the doctors, the solicitors – and with the students. Héloïse classed as student – (whether they were in fact students was of no consequence; if she saw someone even once with a book under his arm, then to address him she would immediately select this sentence with its magical overtones: "Are you perhaps a student, sir?" Frequently, Sir replied that he sold salad at a stand on the market place, but she paid no heed; indulgently, she granted him of her own free will the title "Student") – as students, then, Héloïse classed all those boys who came with untutored eloquence and blushing cheek to visit her in the evening, after six o'clock. There were also visitors who fell under the heading "Old"; others, under the heading "Fat"; and also certain others, who did not fail to excite a feeling of contempt in Héloïse (a feeling of contempt that she found painful, for it was very like the feeling she entertained toward her own family), who came under the heading "Poor." The "Poor," in Héloïse's classification, were those who had nothing to give her, those into whose shirt pockets she was obliged to slip a slice of onion or a piece of bread.

If Mme Octavie Enbonpoint had known! Mme Octavie, who was so thrifty, quite as thrifty certainly as Mother Superior in the convent, counting her pennies, noting down her expenses every evening in her ledger, trembling at the thought of her children going hungry, brooding like a bossy hen over the whole of that large and scattered family that caused her so much worry! Héloïse greeted each of Mme Octavie's sighs with never-failing admiration. As a great ship thrusts aside the waves, so Mme Octavie, with her majestic arms and powerful shoulders, would thrust aside the enormous difficulties that daily surged around her in her house.

"Here, here! I'm coming! What's going on here? They're not to be beaten, do you hear? These girls are protected, the Rose Tavern must keep its good reputation, I'll have no drunks in here! You can drink when you leave. This way, sir. Be a good girl, Gisèle, the gentleman means no harm, he can't hurt you. Up and down the stairs, but I've got a bad heart! Did you know that? I can't sleep like other people, lying in a bed. No, I have to sleep in a chair. Sitting up. What a life! And all day I'm walking, running, flying here and flying there, people calling for me every moment, needing me on every floor, too many stairs, I tell you. And too many rooms, I can't go on with it, you're my witness, there's not a breath left in me!

"But all the same," thought Héloïse, playing with a lock of her hair on her forehead, "Mme Octavie is too fond of wine, and she eats too much cheese. Mother Superior was very fond of cheese too. But she never ate it during Lent. Perhaps Mme Octavie ought to fast also, perhaps she ought to do penance like Mother Superior."

"I don't need your advice," Mme Octavie replied. "I'm three times your age. Think about that. They'll find me stretched out dead at the foot of the stairs one fine morning. And don't send for the priest when they do, if you please. Even if I get down on my knees and beg you to. I shall never forgive him for what he said to me, standing up there in his pulpit, that Abbé Moisan. If you had heard the shameful word he used to describe my business here!

When I have worked so hard! When I have done my duty every day! Though naturally I have my faults, like anyone else."

Héloïse wrote to her grandmother almost every day, reminding her that her granddaughter was now a cook and well rewarded for her services, *provided with good clothes and board and lodging all for nothing dear grandmother* – so I hope you will accept the generous contribution I am sending toward the hospital expenses of my poor invalid brother, for whom you see me shedding tears of desolation and sympathy. God has always tried us cruelly dear grandmother be brave I am thinking of you . . . I am seeing a great many people grandmother night and day and all the time at last I feel I am useful and Mme Octavie Enbonpoint the manager of the tavern and my devoted mistress begs me to tell you that she is very proud of me I am completely in her charge and do all she tells me to don't worry about my not going to Mass dear grandmother . . . Dear sir [she wrote to the town solicitor], your visit brought me great pleasure your absence is killing me you forgot your hat and gloves . . .

"Let us try that sentence again," Mme Octavie broke in, her face inflamed with gluttony (for the smell of roasting veal and mushrooms was floating up to them from the kitchen). Dear sir, in a word, I love you . . . I . . .

Héloïse sat musing, her pen poised in mid-air, her forehead furrowed in thought. Mme Octavie had been so good to her! The day before she left home, Héloïse had drawn a red ring around Mme Octavie's advertisement in the local paper:

Good Wages! Young Girl 18 to 20 wanted!
Maid of all work
Octavie Enbonpoint
The Public Rose Tavern
3 rue de la Bonne-Fortune
Parish of St. Mark of the Thaw

There were also a few other items in the classified column, such as:

Responsible young lady wanted
for old man out of his mind,
Beautiful country Salary once a month
St. Pit's Lane, Route Number 8
(follow the avenue of firs and turn right)

Need nurse
middle height and blue eyes
Single person suffering
from amnesia
(Route Number 2, pinewood cabin)

To take care of children from 1 to 8
As well as young animals
Woman, at least 50 years old
Impatient widower

Héloïse had not known how to choose among all these offers. Were there so many people then, she thought with tears in her eyes, were there so many strangers who needed her? She had immediately thought of rushing to help the old man in St. Pit's Lane, or the widower surrounded by children, in fact all those people whose cries for help had caught her eye in the CLASSIFIED ADVERTISE-MENTS on Saturday (in a paper, moreover, entitled *Around the World in an Hour* – which Monsieur le Curé passed on to Grand-mère Antoinette every Saturday, even though it was already three months out of date when he received it – but Grand-mère Antoinette paid no attention to the date, she read the spring temperatures in winter, perused the list of marriages at a time when one of the newlyweds had already been laid in the earth, and the frightful news of an earthquake or a large-scale fire would always reach her when the earth had long since ceased to tremble and everyone had long forgotten THE 100 DEAD ENGULFED IN A MINUTE who, a few months earlier, had had a certain réclame thanks to their resounding disappearance; she would shed tears over a death-dealing fire that had destroyed whole villages and carried off men, women, and children whom she would never have had the opportunity of seeing, since she never went out except to go to church . . . She prayed for miners buried alive in the farthest regions of the globe, and when she heard of dangerous torrid weather scorching the grass and withering up the harvest in such and such a far-off country, it was not without nostalgia, not without regret, her hands red and chapped with cold, that she turned toward the window – and toward the hill still white with snow, the road lying motionless beneath the trees, the pale sky, the immutable sky of her own destiny – a gaze that expressed her disenchantment with the winter and the monotonous cold).

And so, as she considered each of these misfortunes, Héloïse stretched out her arms, longing to cradle all these unhappy people in her bosom. The Lost Property and Missing Persons columns filled her heart with pity.

Child eight to ten
Black eyes no hair
Highway robber
Hasn't been seen by his mother
For a month
Please return to owner
Punishment will follow

A young girl left her home
One evening after supper

> Blond hair, scar on leg
> Etc. . . .

Being of a serious nature and without a sense of humour, Héloïse never lingered over the comic strips. Scarcely had the paper made its entrance into the house than the elder brothers and their father would fling themselves upon Strange Customs Illustrated, then spend the whole of Sunday morning sitting on the church porch, their pipes in their mouths, hair blowing in the wind, attempting with furious obstinacy to make it yield up its secrets. No. Héloïse allowed herself to read nothing but the Lonely Hearts column, *The Hidden Heart, The Secrets of the Heart, The Confessions of a Loving Heart* – which her grandmother carefully put together for her (always using this miraculous page from the weekly newspaper to wrap up the bread and ham she took up to her granddaughter during the period of her fasts) every Saturday . . .

What sweet joy it was for Héloïse to discover in that important publication so many "hearts betrayed" and "hearts savagely trampled on" that were so very like her own – but what was to be done, o Lord, for the young girl in some remote village

> Who had had a child
> By an unknown father

Or for the teenager Victoline Dubois

> Who had hairs on her chin
> And for this reason
> Had lost the young man she was engaged to.
> I would like a good recipe, please,
> For making me attractive to boys.

Eventually, Mme Octavie Enbonpoint had appealed to Héloïse because of the solidity of her name. And so the morning came when Héloïse began her new life in St. Mark of the Thaw, a village more populous than the one where she was born – "There is at least one extra church," she thought as she saw a pink tower breaking the skyline, and then a general store, in which they sold not only boots, silk stockings, and corsets but also chickens (alive, but they killed them while you waited if you liked), chocolate, pastilles for sore throats, oats, and a thousand other things that to Héloïse were a mark of the village's prosperity – ranging from men's suits (Medium Size) to *Ladies Hosiery* via *Farm Implements and Horse Blankets*. And from the general store one could just make out, bathed in all the joyful frankness of its name,

THE PUBLIC ROSE TAVERN
Dinners at all hours tea coffee
No beer served on Sundays

What good luck for Héloïse, who was about to be greeted by Mme Octavie with open arms and a cry of: "Come in, come in, my child! I was expecting you!" But while Mme Octavie was lavishing on Héloïse a succession of slippers, dresses, and corsets (Oh heavens! how thin you are! take that off at once!), the young girl was forced to admit with a blush that all she knew how to make was soup – pea soup or any sort of soup you liked, but nothing else, Mme Octavie, because you see I spent my youth in the convent, in prayer and meditation, Mme Octavie. Mme Octavie, with a shake of her ample and jewel-hung bosom (Héloïse was so shy that she had not yet dared to raise her eyes and inspect the Manager of the Tavern in her entirety, fearing that her own appearance had been a source of disappointment . . .), announced that praying was not a necessary accomplishment in her house, nor cooking either.

She dared openly, and also unavailingly, since Héloïse in her innocence did not understand a word: "I don't know whether you have noticed the fact, my child, but you are in a brothel; there is still time to go back to the convent if that is what you want. This is no place for little girls."

"But you will have hot water in your bedroom," Mme Octavie continued, not waiting for Héloïse to answer, "and will have your turn in the bathtub too. Every Saturday. You won't need a key for your room. I keep a very careful watch on all the young ladies who live here. Nothing can happen to you. Oh, I forgot to mention that my heart is in a very bad way. Yes, I'm a condemned woman. Anyway, that's what I'm told. Don't forget to bring me around when I lose consciousness. It sometimes happens if I've eaten too much."

Reminded suddenly of her convent days by a sensibility still too conscious of the past, Héloïse decided to take down the lascivious photographs that had been hung all over the walls of her room. Since her eyes were still lowered, Héloïse was unable to make out anything of those naked, crouching figures bathing in the moonlight, offering in the quiet of their white hands, like pairs of lambs in some snowy retreat, immense white breasts, also victims of their own candour, over which, like the chaste locks of the Madonna, there tumbled heavy golden tresses, unsullied symbols, like the breasts, of an innocence about to be lost, a beauty soon to be consecrated in debauchery. Héloïse was unable to make out anything in this depraved fairy landscape but the chaste foot of a girl who was depicted as spurning a pool full of toads – as in other pictures she had seen the Virgin spurn the head of the malignant serpent – but, warned by some vague odour of carnality emanating from the presence of Mme Octavie beside her, she had a feeling that it would be better to replace these pictures with the crucifix from her convent cell – which she did in fact do later on, to the horrified surprise of Mme Octavie, who left the crucifix where it was but stuck the pictures, which she considered necessary to the satisfaction of her clients' appetites, back on the walls beside it.

And as she did so, Mme Octavie supposed herself to be casting anchor in a new and undiscovered sea of sensuality, steering her voyagers toward some mysteriously spasmodic current – labouring without a qualm in her task of creating a pleasant atmosphere in the haven she had built for love.

In her distressing sincerity, Héloïse continued to say her prayers every night, imploring God, just as her mother had done, to dispel her fears; and perhaps the unknown lover, the handsome vagabond in her room, who had come just for a single night, might hear before and after love, without quite understanding them, those hesitant Pater Nosters she was to murmur, lips tightly closed to hide her secret. And perhaps, opening his eyes as a childish hand caressed him in its search for warmth, he would ask:

"What was it you were saying then, while I was asleep?"

And perhaps, she would gently reply: "I think I was saying that I love you." So that before long, though never ceasing to compare life in the Tavern with her happy days spent in the convent, slipping from one form of contentedness into another – just as you can swoon in exactly the same way with either pain or pleasure in a dream, telling yourself that the night is safe around you, that you cannot fall any further than a dream – that the man who is making you bleed in a bed, the man who is cutting off your head and whom nevertheless you can see running off with your head still smiling under his arm, will soon be the same man to whom you grant forgiveness, without a word, with a vague gesture of your arm, of that lost and floating hand you will let fall toward him, or simply for whom the action of expiring, of disappearing into silence is already a memorable sign that the dream will soon be drawing to a close, and that a strange dignity is ordering you to die a second time, quickly, before the blood-thirsty prince who made you melt with such excessive languor comes back again . . . Floating from a happy body into a sad body, from one lover, kind in spite of all his harshness, to another whom she believed she was making love to in the sunlight, lying on warm sand (and yet the bedroom, all this while, was becoming tinier and tinier, the walls shrinking closer and closer together), before long, Héloïse came at last to know the disturbing harmony of a satisfied desire, feeling all the happinesses she had ever know melt into one within her. Héloïse felt her arms loaded with roses, she was running through the novices' garden in the convent, while through a luminous window opening on apple trees there came the voices of the younger nuns singing during recreation . . . One of them was playing the piano, her hand lingering on the melting, airy notes, each joined to the next by a slender thread as fine as rain, and her imagination, now refreshed, revealed to her the joys that were to come. Under a burning summer sun she was singing as she walked along the road with her new friends from the tavern, all in light-coloured dresses and pale straw hats. Or else they were all jumping together, as though in some scented and gigantic cake, in a mountain of hay that was bouncing in the back of a cart, a cart being led by a care-free farmer, his face tanned by the sun, who held the horse's rein with an idle hand . . . Ardent and incurable in her passions, Héloïse did honour to Mme Octavie, who, although she had announced with pride that she wanted no convent girls in her house, had in fact filled it almost with nothing else, from the sulky little girl who still played with her doll as soon as her customers had left (thought Mme Octavie had in fact picked her out of the gutter and was only giving her the benefit of this charitable tutelage until such time . . .), to the young girl with the peasant profile, aged between fifteen and seventeen, who had come to town with the best intentions in the world, "to find a job, Madame, I can wash dishes, look after pigs . . . ," and those who came "just for a moment, Madame, to ask your advice – what dress should I wear at my sister's wedding?" "Come into the boudoir, my child, we can chat there in peace. We can't talk here, there are too many people." Mme Octavie required no particular qualities in her children, nei-ther beauty nor elegance, for she considered it one of her sacred duties to admit the handicapped into her house along with the rest. And this was why she claimed she had a good reputation in spite of everything, and did not deserve the bombastic disdain that was showered down upon her by the Abbé Moisan from his pulpit whenever he saw an opportunity.

"They are orphans, bastards, cripples, and I rescued them from the garbage heap, Monsieur l'Abbé. My charge is as great as yours, and I'm not going to let you tell me otherwise again . . ."

But since the Abbé Moisan had hurled his public curse upon Mme Octavie's *infamous traffic,* the latter, as a tree yields up its ripest fruits at the onslaught of a vigorous gust of wind, had only let fall a more abundant manna upon Mme Octavie's head – which she considered she certainly deserved, after all her efforts. Except in church, where she had been forbidden to set foot, Mme Octavie was cordially greeted everywhere. Everyone commiserated with her on the sad state of her heart ("A very big heart, truly, it rescued me from my husband"): the Mayor lifted his hat when he saw her, in acknowledgement; the Doctor called out, *My respects, Madame,* and quickly crossed the street lest he be observed by any of his patients; the dentist was grateful because she brought so many little girls over to his deserted surgery (and since their teeth were always prematurely dead, he invariably tore them all out and implanted new ones, whose glittering and paralytic smiles were then to be seen, all over town, bearing such charming witness to the whiteness of his products); and even the young men who went to confession every Friday, even they followed Mme Octavie on the street, sniffing unashamedly at the irresistible gusts stirred up by her stiffly starched skirts, drawn along in the wake of sensuality which she always trailed behind her, from the general store to the bank, from the bank to the market . . .

On summer evenings, as he sat smoking outside his house, the Abbé Moisan would follow all this commotion with a frowning glare, promising himself, next time the opportunity arose, to mete out harsher punishment still in his sermons to this accursed woman whom he could see stalking imperiously among the men and boys, shoulders straight, heart lit up with her own importance, and provocative enough, the Abbé Moisan thought to himself, to tumble even the saintliest of men down into hell, simply by raising her little finger . . .

Héloïse was writing to tell the town solicitor that she was in perfect health, that he, M. Laruche, would have no further cause for complaint since the dentist had now replaced all her teeth.

(Don't worry monsieur I didn't suffer Mme Octavie was very brave and held my head there was blood on my arms could you come on Thursday at eight o'clock Mme Octavie sends you sincere greets.) And a few days later M. Laruche the solicitor was waiting in the salon, sitting on the edge of his chair, surrounded by the Young Ladies, who were also sitting on the edges of their chairs, skirts scrupulously raised above their knees, just as Madame had shown them during their initiation period, but pressing their thighs together, all the same, in a sudden rush of modesty appropriate to their childish years. (Though, naturally, M. Laruche's eyes were far too quick not to catch, with a blink of his heavy eyelids, the scarlet flash of a pair of drawers meeting the fresh skin of a delicately shifted thigh.) Beside him, also seated, was Mme Octavie, who on such occasions assumed the dignity of the great wild cats, clad from head to foot in a yellow dress as dazzling as the sun, listening to the sighs, like those of a lioness, escaping from her gold-swathed bosom, and holding tightly against her side the beautiful, cruel hand that she intended to let fall at any moment upon the neck of one of those terrified gazelles – a huntress, but without murderous intent, for M. Laruche (We pay in advance here, dear Monsieur Laruche . . .) would be left to make his kill himself. The Young Ladies, respectful of their company and ignoring the vague stench of tobacco surrounding the solicitor, inhaled the odious smoke from his cigars as little as possible and refrained from frowning with disgust as he spat little pieces of cigar on the floor. ("You must think of this as a second home," Mme Octavie said with a shrug of the shoulders – though this did not prevent her from thinking behind that impassive brow, "But really, what a pig he is!") The Young Ladies, their mouths still fresh from the tortures inflicted on them by the dentist, M. Silex, all curved their lips into courageous smiles. "Like lilies!" M. Laruche exclaimed.

"Like lilies newly opened and waiting to be picked!"

But which one was he to choose? ("Mlle Héloïse would very much like you to go up and visit her, she has a slight headache, so she's lying down on her bed while she waits . . .") "I haven't a great deal of time, I only stopped by to pass the time of day with you, Mme Octavie," the solicitor said, looking at his watch. (From his buttoned waistcoat, over which he was wearing a short corduroy jacket, M. Laruche drew forth his imposing watch, with its silver chain that always filled the heads of the little girls, beneath the hair smoothed down with unguents, beneath the ornaments twined from fading flowers, with pleasant fantasies.) "Let's see, what time is it? I mustn't forget my visit to the Mayor at noon, and then the funeral parlour at one o'clock, and my wife . . ." And with his ever watchful eye, M. Laruche surveyed his firmament of lust. The Young Ladies, so many respectful planets, awaited his decision without moving, hands on knees. From wall to ceiling, thanks to the nymphs and virgins seeming to emerge from the hangings and skip with carefree nudity toward the solicitor's mad debauch, the old man was able to inhale the perfumes of the stars in plenteous profusion, his feet clad in slippers ("Make yourself at home, M. Laruche, make yourself at home"), his dimpled fingers already dallying with the curving form of the moon.

"Héloïse," he suddenly exclaimed, "I'll settle for Héloïse!"

And to the relief of the young ladies sitting half-drugged by the smoke he had pumped into the salon, M. Laruche dragged himself painfully toward the staircase, with Mme Octavie behind him, helping him to climb each step and sighing all the time, *Ah Monsieur Laruche, how old we're getting!*

The solicitor removed his watch but refused to take off his corduroy waistcoat. M. Laruche was in the habit of smoking a cigar in bed, which was not always quite to Héloïse's taste. Sometimes he climbed into the bed without taking off his slippers, another thing that Héloïse did not approve of, though she was far too refined to mention it. M. Laruche had scarcely started to undress Héloïse when he began to lose his breath – and he lost it more and more as he approached the reefs (so that Héloïse could hear nothing, as he continued on his voyage, but distant splashing sounds – how humiliating it would be if M. Laruche were never to return to the surface of that muddy stream, she would have to call for Mme Octavie, and who else besides . . . Oh! how her teeth hurt suddenly, and her jaw where it had been split open, stitched up, and then restitched, and the stone teeth implanted in her still bleeding gums . . .) And without giving a thought to her, M. Laruche the solicitor was continuing his travels imprisoning the young girl's mouth beneath his lips as they frothed with tobacco and sweat, sliding a tactless hand into the delicate folds beneath her arm. (Héloïse moaned so softly that the old man did not hear her, aïe, Monsieur Laruche, aïe . . .) For Héloïse, always inclined to compassion, saw the man now trampling on her youth with no regard for the misery he was inflicting on her body or the loneliness of her desire – saw him as a child, a big baby with primal appetites, suspended from her nipple, exploiting in all kinds of gestures and sudden transports – none of which seemed in any way more ignoble than any other, once a certain stage of frenzy had been reached – the thirst, the huge thirst of that first day, unfortunately unassuaged, that now had the effect of making the man who had come to enjoy the embraces of a mistress desire at the same time the caresses of a mother capable of corrupting him. Cast up on a sterile shore by M. Laruche (standing in the noonday light, his paunch bulging inside his drawers, his watch on the bedside table and a cigar between his teeth, the old man was congratulating himself on having been able to bring things to a conclusion without too great an expense of time, so that he could now sally forth, refreshed and alert from his visit to the brothel, to pay his visit to the Mayor, the Curé . . .), Héloïse was thinking back, without too much distaste, over what had just happened . . .

After the solicitor would come the boys, escaping for an hour or so from school, pushing one another as they waited their turn on the stairs; and Héloïse would simply give them candies and hold their hands, assuming the role of tender accomplice to a curiosity that she herself refused to satisfy, for to her they seemed too candid, too unsullied, these young rogues with bright clear eyes who reminded her of Jean Le Maigre or Number Seven, whom she had also been forced to eject from her bedroom on occasions, when in the leaden light of dawn they came in and surprised her as she lulled the sufferings of her lonely sex with caresses she herself provided, cradling thus in gentle sadness a lover or a mistress (or some vaguely delineated being who would salve the hurts of her wounded imagination) whose face she took pleasure in forgetting, secretly haunted by a shadowy hand belonging to an invisible body. And in the room next door, Marthe-the-Little-Hunchback and Gisèle the orphan would not fail to open their door to the boys standing disappointed on the stairs. They would say to them, as they had to the Jean Le Maigres and the Number Sevens they had welcomed onto their knees in earlier days, in the school playground ("If you tickle me again, I shall tell Mlle Lorgnette." Then, after a moment's reflection: "Go on, do it again, it's such fun, and no one can see us"), though they had grown up a lot since their schooldays, or so they thought, ah! that was all such a long time ago: Ah, they cried as they stood in the doorway, their lips smudged with lipstick, sprightly as squirrels perched up on delicate paws – *do come in and play with us,* Mme Octavie is downstairs, do come in and play with us, no one is here to see . . .

And in a trice the boys had vanished into the room to spend a morning whispering and quivering in the company of their mocking mistresses, who thought only of pulling their hair and aping their grimaces in the mirror, forgetting everything while they played, until Mme Octavie appeared, to interrupt these frolics in indignation, insisting that the boys should pay, and on the spot what's more, the debts incurred on their previous visit (twenty cents an hour or nothing), and saying to the little girls, as Mlle Lorgnette or Mme Casimir might have done, emerging onto the school porch and brandishing a pointer: "Now, now, playtime is over."

Lying downcast upon his bed in the hospital and surrounded by paupers, by casualties admitted that morning (too poor to afford a room of their own and die in peace), by drunks admitted the evening before, all victims of despair in various forms, delirium tremens, madness, or hysteria, Pomme had just fallen from the nest, and like a young bird which has deserted its home before it is strong enough to fly, he lay gazing at the heavy useless wings still quivering slightly at his sides, in dread that he might revive the wound that still hung, or so it seemed to him, from the end of the hand that felt so heavy under its dressing, from the raw extremity of every vanished finger. He wept in silence, his nose reddened by the constant flow of rheum, tears furrowing down from both nostrils, too depressed to use Uncle Armandin's handkerchief that he was holding in his healthy hand with an air of one about to set out on a journey, to make a sad farewell, even though he was lying motionless in bed. In the beds on either side, two drunks lay bewailing their lot; farther off, a woman who had recently been brought in after falling off a roof was spewing out invective against her absent husband. Pomme, there could be no doubt about it, was in hell. The minutes flowed by with infinite slowness, and Pomme, tormented by an invisible executioner, was suffering, suffering with much less courage than his brother Jean Le Maigre had shown on his deathbed, but with the same patience his mother might have shown in giving birth to one of her children.

He called for his grandmother, for his father, for his mother, for all his family, all buried beneath the snow, so far away – he called out all their names in a whisper, one after the other: Anita Aurelia Roberta Héloïse oh! Héloïse – he made a gentle chant of his despair, his head in the hollow of his pillow, his hands on the sheets like the hands of a mummy. And all this while, bloated after a satisfying meal, Uncle Armandin Laframboise was playing cards with his sturdy wife, who, separated from him by a screen of saucepans that had not yet been cleared away, was murmuring in boredom, without even bothering to open her mouth: "Armandin, is that a club? That means you haven't got a heart . . . ."

And Number Seven was wandering through the streets, hands in his pockets, hair blowing in the wind, ready to throw stones through a few windows, the recent victor in a pretty tough snowball fight with the Neighbourhood Gang, his eyes full of devilry, and encouraged by the thought of his thin cheeks, which gave him that tough look he needed to confront the bigger members of the Terror Squad, who were lying in wait for him on the right, and the smaller fry of the Army of the Rue de Champs, who always waited for him to emerge from the factory at the end of the day – though still more encouraged, to be sure, by the star-shaped battle scar on his eyelid and an intoxicated awareness of the knife slashes across his brow. Number Seven was going to keep a rendezvous with a friend who often waited for him in the evening under the snow-covered arches of the alley. Number Seven puffed out his chest under his coat as he walked, just as Uncle Armandin did when he got up in the morning, before washing himself thoroughly in front of the open window – his day had been so long and the hour at which he rose so premature, as premature as that of the cocks, that Number Seven was yawning indefatigable as he walked. Ah, yes! He was a man already. Like a man he rose at dawn, set out for the factory with his satchel on his back, and arrived there first so as to earn the praises of his boss. Though naturally the boss didn't have time to notice him. Like God in the catechism book, he was inaccessible to little folk. But fortunately there was the secretary. And the secretary, as everybody knew, was full of compassion for the weak. He was a good and tolerant man. Pomme therefore had no reason to complain about losing his fingers in the innocent blades of a machine! The secretary was not responsible for lost property. Pomme cut out soles, and Number Seven glued them on. The machines, according to the secretary, were reputed to be as rapid and precise as lightning. Like lightning, they hurtled magically downward 1,700 times each day as they stamped out the leather for

126

the shoes, controlled, it goes without saying, by the deserving work-man who contributed to their operation. Dazzled by these words, Number Seven stuck on his soles with ardour. Though little by lit-tle, all the same, he began to compare them with innumerable heads being chopped off by a guillotine. 1,000 heads, 1,001 heads . . . Once executed, they were passed swiftly on to the next execu-tioner, who hardly glanced at them, having seen so very many.

The secretary was walking quickly up and down between the lines of workers. He had on a grey suit with a white necktie and was afraid of dirtying his hands in that dust-filled jungle. Number Seven was sticking on his 1200th pair of soles as fast as he could, his nose and eyes filled with the black sparkling dust. What a pity the secretary could not see how well he was doing his job, for the secretary was nearsighted . . .

Hands in pockets, Number Seven was finished with the fac-tory until tomorrow, and he was now breathing in the cool evening air, eyes raised to the star-filled sky. A mountain of leather soles moved with him, but he shoved them aside with one elbow, as he might indolently have repulsed some enemy in a dream.

Latin Greek Natural Science
Arithmetic
Young men from families of modest means
1 rue du bon air
THEO CRAPULA TUTOR

Number Seven was going to meet Brother Théodule. Slyly insinuating himself into Number Seven's destiny like a serpent into a silken nest, Théo Crapula had come to rescue the young lad, to guide him in all honour along the path of virtue. Number Seven followed Brother Théodule to the latter's grimy den. He thanked his grandmother for having placed him under the tutor's divine protection. (Dear Madame, My superior is sending me into the town, where I am to conduct a mission for several days. Perhaps you would allow me to keep an eye on your grandson, Fortuné-Mathias . . . I am at your entire and devoted disposal . . . The temptations that threaten youth today . . . The child is in need of moral guidance . . . If you will be good enough to give me his address . . . etc. . . . To which Grand-mère Antoinette enthusiastically replied:

For the orphan
A father has been found
Thank you oh Lord)

And so Number Seven realized that he was to be given the opportunity of making up all that time he had so shamefully wasted on his bench at school in younger days – begging from Brother Théodule, who was, it should be added, as ignorant as the man in the moon, a few crumbs of Latin, Greek, and above all spelling, that the wind was destined to scatter again immediately, since Number Seven had formed the intention of living honestly in the future on what he could steal.

A bristling, dirty beard disfiguring his cheeks, his eyes yellow with fatigue, Brother Théodule did not seem to be listening to the monotonous little voice reciting its lessons by his side. They were of no concern to him, those hundred sheep that had been bought or sold, that total of goats or cabbages Number Seven was searching for, nibbling the end of his pencil as Jean Le Maigre had always done in the same circumstances, his gaze a thousand miles from the problem. No, Brother Théodule was thinking about something else: he was brooding over his disappointment, and entirely forgetting the presence of Number Seven in his room. Astonished that Brother Théodule was not asking him any questions, Number Seven thought of trying to make up problems for himself. He knew the price you had to pay if you wanted consideration and good humour from Monsieur Théo Crapula. He was used to it.

"We might perhaps go for a walk in the moonlight," Théo Crapula said in feeble tones. "I feel a little unwell this evening . . ."

Number Seven closed his exercise book. Farewell, sheep and goats; once again the class was coming to an end too soon. Number Seven resigned himself to the thought of gluing on soles all his life, he who had dreamed of writing novels like his brother, of playing the organ like Monsieur le Curé, of singing in a choir like the novices at Jean Le Maigre's funeral! He would never learn to play the piano now. "An impossible dream," his grandmother had written to him. "We are only poor folk. You must give up these dreams of grandeur, child." But he consoled himself with visiting the various churches on Sunday morning; he listened to the choir of young girls in Notre-Dame de la Pitié, and stood at the foot of the porch outside the church of Saint-Paul sniffing in the smell of incense, lulled with delight by the murmuring thunder of the organ that came, it seemed to him, from heaven. He waited impatiently for the trumpets of the Last Judgment, the bugles of celestial victory, and then, in calmer moments, dreamed of hearing the Christmas shepherds' humble flutes.

"We might walk down by the river, under the bridge," Brother Théodule said . . .

Sunday mornings passed then, for Number Seven, in religious fervour and communion. He communicated at each church in turn, and the host sticking to his teeth would fortify him with its symbolic power. He poured floods of holy water over his head, both before and after Mass, and when he took his turn as acolyte, one Friday in each month, he drank the Communion wine and dipped his fingers in Christ's blood with tight-shut eyes. He wanted to become better, to sanctify himself, to recover for a moment that state of grace which in him, alas, was as ephemeral as the rose and became tarnished at the slightest contact. He said his prayers every evening kneeling at the foot of his bed, and asked that Jean Le Maigre might enjoy good health in the other world.

"Come," Brother Théodule said, opening the door into the cold night. Attracted perhaps by the smell of rotting wood from the nearby river, a rat could be seen gliding off across the snow. It was a clear night and Number Seven was gay, in spite of his weariness. Silently, Théo Crapula guided him toward the bridge, pressing his long hand on the young boy's shoulder, as though he were afraid of falling over as he walked. He had turned up his coat collar, and Number Seven could scarcely see his face in the glow from the street lamps. He was still smoking nervously, and his hand trembled on Number Seven's shoulder. The least noise in the street, the slightest shimmer from a lamp or from a window, or the imperceptible touch of a stranger brushing past seemed to fill him with uneasiness. Drawing Number Seven nearer to the wall, he climbed distrustfully down toward the river.

"Wheuu . . . wheuu . . ." Number Seven whistled, hands in pockets ("No, no, don't whistle," Brother Théodule implored in a pitiable voice, "I beg of you, don't whistle . . ."), thinking that spring was coming at last, that the flowers would soon begin to bud again in his grandmother's garden (a garden the size of a pocket handkerchief, Grand-mère Antoinette used to say, but with what fastidious care she always tended it, at dawn, her big watering can in her hand, her hair tied back under a nightcap, like a nun who has just got out of bed) – Number Seven fell silent. He had seen the machine again, the machine that killed Pomme's fingers. Plock . . . plock . . . plock, oh! that bleeding crown of fingers falling beneath the axe. (With its unfeeling blade, the machine continued to cut out soles, and as it sank its steel into the leather it was slicing into flesh, plock . . . plock . . . "The 500th pair of boots," the secretary said. "Don't stop. These things happen.")

Pomme had fainted. Nobody seemed to have seen him fall, crumbling gently into the dust.

"I do wish I could go home," Number Seven said, quite suddenly. "Yes, I wish I were somewhere else, I feel a little sick inside."

But suddenly the noise stopped. There was only the sound of Pomme's breathing as he lay on the floor. Only the sound of his heart beating in the machine, now that it had stopped. "What a nuisance," the director said, "call the doctor quickly." "A day lost," the secretary in the white necktie said. "If you don't mind, I'll go and wash my hands."

"His name, do you know his name?"

"It's in our files, monsieur."

Pomme disappeared along a white corridor, wheeled on a stretcher by some nuns. Uncle Armandin had taken off his hat, Number Seven took off his hat as well.

"Well, that's how it is," Uncle Armandin said with a shrug. "That'll teach him to daydream when he's supposed to be cutting out shoes, eh? I always said it wasn't for him, the factory. Better to send him to a bakery some place. He ate up all my wife's cakes!"

The river was calm and luminous. Brother Théodule turned down his coat collar and took a deep breath, suddenly relieved of his anxiety.

"What a beautiful night it is," he said to Number Seven, who wasn't listening. "Do you know the name of that star up there? I could teach it to you . . . I could teach you a great many things if you wanted!"

So, Number Seven thought, at last he's made up his mind what it is he wants from me. No, he thought obstinately, I don't want to see the star he's telling me about. I don't want to know its name. I don't like looking at the sky, not this evening.

"But you'll give me some chocolates, a whole box, won't you? My brother Pomme is in the hospital. It's not for myself I'm asking, monsieur . . ."

"I'll give you everything you want," Théo Crapula answered, "yes, everything, but let me tell you something first . . ."

And Théo Crapula described a dream he had dreamed the night before.

"You were whipping me, yes, you were whipping me till you were in a frenzy, and I was happy, I asked you to whip me more . . . You were my judge, my master . . ."

Number Seven began to yawn again.

"It's not my fault if you have bad dreams, monsieur. There's nothing cruel about me, I don't like killing flies, I never tear the wings off butterflies, I'd never whip you, monsieur. No," he went on in a gentle voice, "never, monsieur, even if you were to ask me."

"But I do ask you," Théo Crapula replied, clumsily unfastening his belt. "There is no one else, please, I beg you, do it for me . . ."

Scarcely had Théo Crapula uttered these words, allowing his shabby little passion to soar away on the wings of madness, than Number Seven was running away as fast as his legs could carry him, grazing his knees as he leaped over the piles of rotting wood that lay along the shore like so many wrecks, longing with all the strength of his despair to run farther, and farther, still, to climb back up to the peaceful, well-lit street, where he could call someone to his rescue – for it seemed to him that Théo Crapula's sinister words still reverberated in his ear, like a sentence of death, and that he would not be able to escape from it, or have the courage to howl out the fear that mingled with his tears inside of him – by knocking on Uncle Armandin's door, or on the windows of some stranger's house. Grandma, Mother, he yelled as he ran, and he could hear a train as it passed through the silence of the town, and farther off a church bell chiming nine o'clock, just as it always did. Slowly his fear began to lessen, the pain in his belly little by little began to fade. He was safe, he thought. He could see the bridge. He would soon be there. Théo Crapula was chasing after him with panting cries: "I beg of you . . . don't be afraid . . . I won't hurt you . . ." A hand clutched at Number Seven's shoulder, but he scarcely felt it, so full was his mind of the triumph soon to be his, when he reached the iron staircase leading up to the bridge. Two violent hands were hooking themselves around him, and Number Seven sensed that he was lost. He let himself fall unresistingly upon the sand.

Number Seven awoke at dawn. He was alone on the sandy shore. The sun was rising over the river. He rubbed his eyes. He wasn't dead, as he had thought. His clothes were scarcely torn. But putting his hand up to his neck, he felt a mark that still burned as he touched it.

A season in Emmanuel's life had passed. The snow was beginning to melt, and it was spring. Emmanuel sat up joyfully in his cradle to watch the sun streaming in through the window.

Pomme had been discharge from the hospital. He was walking between his uncle and Number Seven along a street in the town. It was a beautiful March day, but Pomme wasn't looking up at the sky.

"It's a good trade, selling newspapers," Uncle Armandin was saying as he shook his nephew's shoulder. "It's what I've always said, my lad, you don't think enough about the future."

Number Seven was walking in silence, preoccupied with all the bicycles and car headlights he was going to steal. Without doubt he would end up in prison, as his father had so often told him. He no longer had any hope of finding a cure for his need to steal. He had gone too far to turn back now. He was afraid of losing his job in the factory.

But Grand-mère Antoinette had taken Emmanuel in her arms and was whispering in his ear. "Everything is going well," Grand-mère Antoinette told him, "we mustn't lose heart. It's been a hard winter, but the spring will be better. We must thank heaven that Héloïse sends us a little money every week!" Emmanuel clapped his hands. "Yes, everything is going well," Grand-mère Antoinette said, nodding her head in satisfaction.

Pomme hid his mutilated hand inside his jacket. "Head up," Uncle Armandin said to him. "You've got to be brave, eh? You're a man now!"

Emmanuel wasn't cold any more. The sun was shining on the land. A tranquil warmth was flowing through his veins as his grandmother rocked him in her arms. Emmanuel was emerging from the dark.

"Yes, it'll be a fine spring," Grand-mère Antoinette said, "but Jean Le Maigre won't be with us this year . . ."

PORTRAITS OF HÉLOÏSE [1]

An essay on *A Season in the Life of Emmanuel*
by Kirsty Bell

Text and illustration, pieces of the same mosaic, both aim to bring meaning to light.[2]

Since its publication in 1965, Marie-Claire Blais' *A Season in the Life of Emmanuel* has been widely praised by critics and crowned with France's *Prix Médicis* (1966), inspiring numerous studies. The story, both comic and sombre, presents the members of a large Québécois family overseen by the formidable figure of Grand-Mère Antoinette. The novel begins with the birth of the sixteenth child, Emmanuel, but the story focuses largely on the other children: Jean Le Maigre, poet, rebel, and consumptive; Number Seven, a thief with a talent for numbers; and Héloïse, a postulant turned prostitute. At once realistic and fantastic, the fictional world confuses vice and virtue, dreams and reality. The novel also parodies the *roman de la terre* and satirizes the traditional Catholic and conservative mores that dominated Québec before the 1960s. At the same time, the themes of *A Season in the Life of Emmanuel* are universal and resonate in the Western collective imagination.

---

[1] This essay is a translation and adaptation of my article "Portraits d'Héloïse dans l'édition illustrée d'*Une Saison dans la vie d'Emmanuel.*" *Visions poétiques de Marie-Claire Blais.* Eds. Janine Ricouart and Roseanna Dufault. Montréal: Éditions du Remue-Ménage, 2008: 52-69.

[2] Gérard Gréverand. "L'Illustration des *Fables* de la Fontaine, 1668-1980." *Iconographie et littérature. D'un art à l'autre.* Ed. Alain Niderst. Paris: Presses universitaires de France, 1983: 91. All translations of secondary source material are my own.

Despite the success of the novel itself, there has been surprisingly little attention paid to the illustrated edition of *A Season in the Life of Emmanuel*, with its original drawings by Mary Meigs.[3] By analyzing how the illustrations illuminate Blais' story, we can gain an understanding of the double construction – literary and pictorial – of fictional characters. The visual portraits of Héloïse in particular, examined in light of her literary representations, offer a new way of appreciating Blais' novel.

FUNCTIONS OF THE ILLUSTRATIONS

Meigs' India ink drawings first appeared in a special edition of *A Season in the Life of Emmanuel*, published in 1968 by *Éditions du Jour* (three years after the first, non-illustrated novel) with a print run of 500 copies. The large format book (13 inches by 10) is a boxed, deluxe edition including 35 original illustrations by Meigs, each one mounted on brown Mayfair paper, 32 of which are integrated into the novel and three are in a pocket at the end of the book. With the exception of the cover, all of the plates are in black and white and are accompanied by an explanatory legend.[4] In 1972, *Éditions du Jour* released a larger print run of an attractive adaptation of the deluxe edition, with 32 illustrations. This time, the black and white cover art reproduces, in reduced size, one of the pocket illustrations from the special edition (an image that does not

---

[3] Mary Meigs was born in Philadelphia in 1917. She was a successful painter, writer, and activist. She and Marie-Claire Blais met in Massachusetts in the 1960s, lived together in Wellfleet and in Montréal for a number of years, and remained close until Meigs' death in 2002. Meigs discussed her relationship with Blais in her 1981 autobiography *Lily Briscoe: A Self-Portrait*. In addition to the illustrations she developed for *A Season in the Life of Emmanuel*, Meigs also created images inspired by Blais' novels *Nights in the Underground, The Manuscripts of Pauline Archange* and *St. Lawrence Blues*.

[4] The cover image is a colour enlargement of one of the 32 illustrations.

otherwise appear in the second edition). Other than the omission of the two other pocket illustrations, the images and the captions are the same as in the deluxe edition. However, instead of mounting the illustrations, the plates of the adaptation are printed on orange paper. Many features decorate both of these editions: the typography, the italics, the legends, and the coloured dropped capitals at the beginning of each chapter. Thanks to the interaction of text, illustrations, and decorative elements, these illustrated editions are veritable works of art.[5]

In one of the rare reviews of the illustrations for *A Season in the Life of Emmanuel*, Guy Robert notes that Meigs' drawings are "of a brutality, a violence [and] a starkness" that correspond to the "tragic nudity" of Blais' novel.[6] The numerous conformities between the illustrations and the story are evident: the illustrations aim to reproduce the various themes and atmospheres of the novel. The violence and the macabre side of the novel reappear in the portraits of the father and in the representation of Number Seven's rape by Théo Crapula, to cite only two examples. At the same time, the illustrations neglect neither the illusory and unreal aspects of the story nor its grotesque and carnavalesque nature; Jean Le Maigre's and Héloïse's dreams play a role, as do the caricatured portraits of the father, the Confessor and Léopold. In yet other drawings, Meigs transposes moments of tenderness, humour, gentleness, and pleasure. Following a principle of condensation, the series of 35 illustrations can therefore be understood as a diegetic and thematic microcosm of Blais' fictional world.

---

[5] Roger Lacasse claimed that this publication was "the first entirely Canadian volume, thanks to its paper and its typography" and that its launch represented "an important date in the history of Canadian graphic arts." The typographical character, Cartier, used in this edition is a Canadian creation. R. Lacasse. "Un livre de grand luxe relié et imprimé à Québec lancé sous peu." *L'Action Québec* (December 16, 1968): 7.

[6] Guy Robert. "Une Saison violente." *Vie des arts* 58 (1970): 109.

The richness of Meigs' portraits comes largely from the fact that her stylization, the frequent absence of perspective, the use of incongruous proportions, and the deformation of bodies and faces all contribute to an unrealistic aesthetic. Almost all of the illustrations introduce washes of ink that form diffuse stains rather than distinct zones. The superposition of a character and a wash of ink frequently adds an effect of unreality or of dreamlike state to the drawings. Although Meigs' drawings are figurative, they are not part of a realistic approach, a mode of figuration often linked to imitation, mimesis, representation using perspective, and faithful rendering of human anatomy. On the other hand, Meigs' drawings are effective and significant because they play on symbolism, stylization, distortion, and intangibility; their anti-mimetic style attains a high degree of expressive intensity that permits the evocation of atmospheres and themes that are sombre and serene, macabre and joyous, grotesque and serious.

Despite the similarities between the story and the illustrations, Meigs' plates do not constitute an exact reproduction of Blais' novel. The repetition of one scene in two different media, that is to say the "translation" of words into images, supposes shifts in form, strategy, content, and meaning.[7] Through omissions, additions, and stylistic choices, the illustrator transmits her own vision of the novel, a vision that does not escape a definite subjectivity. In other words, depending on the interpretation of the artist, an illustration can be either a faithful transposition of the story or not; it can imitate or deform, elucidate or obfuscate. Illustrations can, in this way, maintain multiple relationships with the story, from conflicting to complementary.

---

[7] In terms of quantity, there are not enough illustrations to present a complete or definitive vision of the story. The 35 images from the deluxe edition are certainly not able to reveal every moment, event or thought described in the novel.

The novel introduces Héloïse at the beginning of chapter three: "Homesick for those protective walls" of the convent, she is still wearing her rigid postulant's dress even though she is at her family home (p. 23). Her excessive piety is evident in the references to her crucifix, her fasting, and her love of sacrifice. Hence a sanctification of this character by her family: Grand-Mère Antoinette likes to remind the village priest that she has a saint at home (p. 24). From the very first presentation of this character, the novel encourages comparisons between Héloïse and the saints: with her crown of thorns, Héloïse resembles martyred saints and with her fasts and her sleepless nights, she subscribes to the asceticism of the mystics.[8]

Héloïse's devotion has, in fact, two remarkable characteristics. Firstly, her asceticism reveals a strong masochistic tendency: she takes pleasure in pain, as her convent name – Sister Héloïse of the Martyrs and of the Blood Shed for Christ – testifies. Since physical love is scorned or even forbidden by the Church and by the family, Héloïse replaces it with the pain of her fasting, her pinpricked fingers, and her crown of thorns. Her religious zeal demands brutal deprivations. Such acts may constitute an attempt to forget her pain and to replace the physical sensations that she misses. Her religious devotion becomes so intense that it resembles sexual ecstasy: "That same night, Héloïse lay pining on a strange bridal bed. She was languishing with desire beside her cruel Bridegroom" (p. 77). Héloïse dreams of a "brutal ravisher" and of rape by an "avenging Bridegroom" (p. 78). Similar to her penchant for masochism, such ecstasies are intimately connected to both pain and sexuality. In this way, the novel constructs a character who aims to fill a psychological or emotional void through masochism and violent sexual fan-

---

[8] Dominique Bourque. "Héloïse ou la voix du silence dans *Une saison dans la vie d'Emmanuel.*" *Voix et images* 23, 68 (Winter 1998): 339.

tasy. Héloïse remains devout throughout the novel, even if religion does not succeed in meeting her needs. Informed as it is by satire and caricature, Blais' novel creates the vision of a pitiful young woman seeking love.

AN EROTICIZATION OF HÉLOÏSE

On the other hand, Meigs' illustrations evoke neither Héloïse's sacred dimension nor her masochistic tastes, but they do produce an eroticization of Héloïse that exposes a positive rendering of female sexuality. The drawings of the young woman's body show the extent to which Meigs' choices inform the significance of the character. The novel describes a thin body, abandoned breasts, a candid belly, and a fine face: "[a]lthough still very young, Héloïse was already dried up like a dead twig" (p. 25); "as she was well aware, her body had been filled with too much suffering by her fasts, made too ugly by curious tortures, for her to feel herself truly a Bride" (p. 78). The illustrations, however, highlight an awakened sexuality: the young woman's body is voluptuous and her breasts are always exposed. It is Héloïse's nudity (partial or complete) that identifies her in the drawings.

Meigs has developed two pairs of illustrations to represent Héloïse: two plates show the dreams she has while at the convent (Chapter VI) and two show her at the the Public Rose Tavern (Chapter VII). The organizational principle of these four drawings is based on a depiction of Héloïse that shows her transition from convent to brothel. Not one illustration depicts her in her religious vestments. Her sensuality and sexuality are predominant.

Incidentally, sensuality is evoked by the luxurious decor that surrounds Héloïse in these drawings. The curves and contours create a lavish milieu in the convent and in the brothel: in the convent, the altar is sculpted and the walls are covered with wallpaper;

in the brothel, the wallpaper is ornate and the floor seems to be covered with a carpet. Contrary to the other largely dark and shaded illustrations of the family home, the school and the noviciate (where no decorative elements are visible), the spaces associated with Héloïse are characterized by their sumptuousness and sensuality.

In the two drawings that show Héloïse in the convent, Meigs has chosen to recreate the desires and dreams of the character. The first dream evokes a life other than that of a nun. This drawing shows the supine, transparent form of Héloïse in front of a group of dancing nuns, their wimples abandoned (figure 1).

Figure 1. *Her confessor interrupted this gush of well-being...*

If shadows and darkness dominate this composition, it is to juxtapose them with the light and transparent silhouette of Héloïse. The tension between light and dark underscores Héloïse's luminosity, to the extent that she has become a diaphanous figure. Her transparency, an aesthetic strategy, provides a more complete picture of the nuns' unusual and animated festivities going on behind her sleeping figure. Her body seems to melt into the bodies of the other women. Because of her diaphanous figure, when Héloïse caresses herself, she also seems to touch the nun's leg (in the centre of the composition). In both the illustration and the novel, the other nuns constitute an object of desire for Héloïse. This drawing shows that the dreamer and the subject of the dream are the same.

In this dream, the Confessor surveys the women's unbridled activities. The very dark depiction of this man is a striking contrast to Héloïse's luminous transparency. Since the Confessor's body is almost indistinguishable from the black background of this drawing, his character is presented as a static figure whose caricatured face symbolizes his aversion to the women's joyous celebrations. The Confessor, whom Meigs depicts as a middle-aged man, casts a disapproving look on the sleeping figure of Héloïse. He becomes a ridiculous character because his severity seems unreasonable in response to the women's very obvious joy. The movement and dynamism of supple female bodies, translated in the composition by the curved lines of the dancing nuns and the rounded form of Héloïse, accentuate their joy.

Furthermore, contrary to what the caption suggests, Héloïse's dream in the picture is not interrupted. The tranquil young woman caresses herself (and at the same time a nun's leg) with a slight smile on her lips. The religious institution (represented by the Confessor) is not able to destroy this moment of pleasure. Religion is also evoked in this illustration by the crucifix attached to the wall. Significantly, though, the head of the crucifix goes beyond the illustration's frame. This "decapitation" depersonalizes the figure of Christ and offers a comment on the inability of the Church to completely stifle the desire shown by these nuns who are dancing light-heartedly and by Héloïse who dreams of finding love. In short, through oppositions between the austerity of the other décors and the luxury of the convent, between the caricature of the Confessor and Héloïse's peaceful expression, between the rigidity of the Confessor and the dynamism of the women and finally between the impotence of religious symbols and the force of the dream, this illustration succeeds in evoking a positive aspect of female pleasure and sexuality.

The second illustration depicting Héloïse in the convent establishes a striking parallel with the first. Once again lying down and nearly naked, Héloïse touches her breasts and her thigh. Her smile unambiguously reveals her pleasure (figure 2).

Figure 2. *This time the convent had been transformed into a joyful tavern...*

Like the Confessor, the Mother Superior surveys her convent, transformed into a place of celebration. Refusing realistic representation by offering a deformation or an exaggeration of traits, Meigs has given the Mother Superior a caricatured face that mocks her and questions her authority. In addition, Héloïse's light figure once again creates a remarkable contrast with the greys and blacks used for the other characters. This time however, with the exception of the Mother Superior, there is no religious symbol. The absence of the crucifix signals that the religious institution has failed in its mission to prohibit sexual love.

There is virtually no transition between these two images of the convent and the two illustrations of Héloïse in the brothel. Read consecutively, the four illustrations suggest that Héloïse goes straight from the convent to the Public Rose Tavern. In the novel, however, the young woman returns to her family home which she then, out of boredom, decides to leave. The drawings' omission of this stage emphasizes the importance of Héloïse's dreams in her passage from convent to brothel. In other words, the illustrations throw light on the realization of dreams. Moreover, no plate associates Héloïse with the family home. She is depicted as an independent woman who engages in sexual acts out of pleasure and not out of boredom or despair. While Jean Le Maigre's prophecies announce a cruel destiny and a depraved life for his sister, Héloïse's life as it is represented in Mary Meigs' illustrations, is untroubled.

The two brothel illustrations portray Héloïse with a client. In the first image, Héloïse is yet again represented naked and lying on her back (figure 3). The rumpled sheets clearly mark the recent sexual act. If Héloïse is not smiling here, as she is in the two pictorial representations of her dreams, she is nonetheless serene. Her calm face and relaxed body indicate that she has satiated her sexual appetite and has even attained a certain emotional satisfaction.

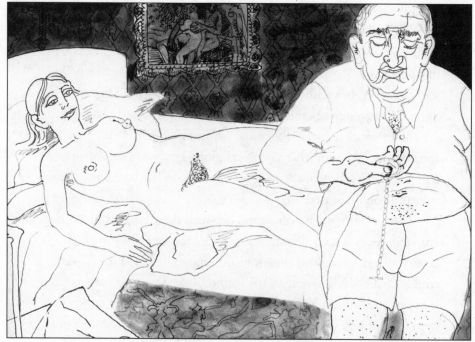

Figure 3. *The old man was congratulating himself on having been able to bring things to a conclusion without too great an expense of time...*

Such fulfilment is hardly evident in the novel, where Héloïse seems more resigned to her work as a prostitute. The novel specifies that Héloïse discovers "the disturbing harmony of a satisfied desire" (p. 117) where the adjective "disturbing" attenuates the peace and harmony that she finds at the Public Rose Tavern. In addition, the novel's description of the sexual relation between Héloïse and her client, the notary, is not an erotic or sensual love scene: the notary kisses her "without giving a thought to her" and "imprisoning the young girl's mouth beneath his lips as they frothed with tobacco and sweat" (p. 122). Héloïse feels compassion for the notary, but the text does not describe her pleasure. Her rapport with the sexual act is ambivalent at best: "Héloïse was thinking back, without too much distaste, over what had just happened..." (p. 123).

The notary is much older than the young prostitute. The portrait of him is certainly mocking, but Meigs does not depict him as a grotesque or sinister character (especially if compared to the drawings of the other adult male characters: the Confessor, the father, or Théo Crapula). In terms of the form or composition of the illustration, the dominant obscurity of the convent gives way here to the lightness of the brothel. Indeed, white dominates almost the entire image and even the client is a light-coloured figure. So the figure of the notary, if not positive, is at least more or less neutral, even if this is not the case in the novel. As for Héloïse, she does not demonstrate any shame or modesty; she even has a confident look.

Behind Héloïse, the lascivious images to which the novel alludes are affixed to the wall. At her arrival at the Tavern, Héloïse removes these photographs in order to display her crucifix. Madame Octavie replaces the pornographic images, hoping to excite her clients' desires, but does leave the crucifix. According to Henri Mitterand, the juxtaposition of Christ and the licentious images constitutes more than a simple commentary on Héloïse's religious and erotic vigour: "The figure of Christ placed between the obscene images denounces a fundamental dupery, the peaceful coexistence, or even complicity of two places where the woman is both queen and slave, under the watch and control of men: the Church and the brothel."[9] There is no suggestion, however, of female slavery in the drawings. While Heloïse is subject to the gaze of her client, the Héloïse in the drawings is motivated by her own pleasure and does not even seem preoccupied with her appearance. Her voluptuous body does not in fact entirely correspond to a western ideal of female beauty since it is not depilated. She does not change anything about her body to seduce or be seduced. It may seem a trivial detail, but Héloïse's body hair suggests that even

---

[9] Henri Mitterand. "Coup de pistolet dans un concert: *Une Saison dans la vie d'Emmanuel*." *Voix et Images* 2, 3 (1977): 414.

though she may be an object of sexual desire for her clients, she is so according to her own conditions.

Furthermore, in the illustrations, Héloïse is able not only to overcome the demands of her work, but also to control her activities and even her clients. The critic Madeleine Greffard does not find any trace of this characteristic in *A Season in the Life of Emmanuel* and proposes that the young woman, "blinded but good [...] is a victim."[10] In the novel, Blais creates a naive character who does not fully realize what she is doing when she arrives at Madame Octavie's. But Héloïse does later reveal a definite awareness: when the young students come to her, she offers them candies and holds their hand. Against all expectation, Héloïse does not make love with them since they are too similar to her brothers Jean Le Maigre and Number Seven (see illustration on page 123).

If the novel suggests in this way that Héloïse makes her own decisions, the final illustration of the prostitute explicitly shows that she controls her situation. She is not portrayed as being compromised by the desires or demands of her clients. The last drawing even evokes a certain calm and sensual intimacy with the boys. Her breast exposed, Héloïse smiles while tenderly looking at the client who is holding her in his arms. She has discovered the admiration and the love that she wanted for so long. Outside the room, the boys waiting on the landing cannot hide their joy. Meigs creates a vision of the prostitute that transcends woman as sexual object or even young woman in search of love. If the playful side of lust is evident in this illustration of Héloïse and her young clients, the images also reveal a woman who is proud of her sexuality, who manages her profession, and who fulfils her thirst for love.

This illustration confirms that Héloïse is also free from the grasp of the Church. A former postulant, she is no longer subject

---

10 Madeleine Greffard. "*Une Saison dans la vie d'Emmanuel*, kaléidoscope de la réalité québécoise." *Les Cahiers de Sainte-Marie* 1 (1966): 22.

to the rules of this institution. Although the cross and the porno-graphic images are visible in the portrait of Héloïse and the notary, the cross is absent in the illustration showing Héloïse and her young clients. Even though Héloïse remains pious throughout the novel, the final pictorial representation of the young woman signals a disappearance of all religious symbols in favour of pleasure.

A brief comparison with other illustrated scenes accentuates the positive representation of Héloïse's sexuality. As in Blais' novel, Meigs demonstrates that the sexual relations between the father and the mother are completely governed by masculine will (and even violence) and have nothing to do with female desire. But Meigs denounces sexual misery with the greatest force in the most troubling of her 35 illustrations – the one in which Théo Crapula rapes Number Seven (figure 4).

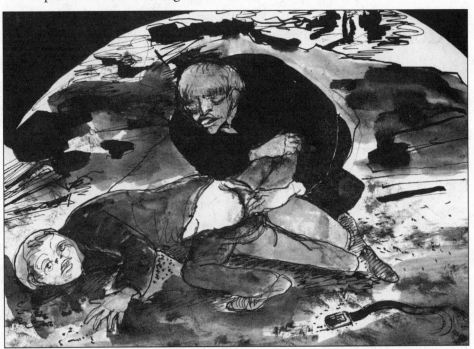

Figure 4. *Two violent hands were hooking themselves around him, and Number Seven sensed that he was lost…*

The novel describes the moment in the following way:

> Théo Crapula was chasing after him with panting cries: "I beg of you... don't be afraid... I won't hurt you..." A hand clutched at Number Seven's shoulder, but he scarcely felt it, so full was his mind of the triumph soon to be his, when he reached the iron staircase leading up to the bridge. Two violent hands were hooking themselves around him, and Number Seven sensed that he was lost. He let himself fall unresistingly upon the sand (p. 133).

In the illustration, the act is just as sinister. Around Number Seven and Crapula there are masses and formless patches of ink, as well as lines and abstract points. In this way, the composition translates the anguish of the victim and the upheaval around him. Even more than the novel, this illustration presents a terrifying, macabre, and nightmarish image of pederasty. It is very clearly a condemnation of sexual abuse of youth by figures of authority, even by priests.

As indisputable antitheses of Number Seven's rape, the four illustrations depicting Héloïse are in fact among the most positive of the 35 drawings in the whole series. From a formal perspective, sexuality and nudity are associated with lighter tones; in their turn, the whiteness and transparency of Héloïse's naked body symbolize contentment. Through the visual recreation of Héloïse's fantasies and the portrayal of her naked, voluptuous body, *eros* becomes the dominant dimension of her character. While the descriptions of Héloïse in the novel evoke an iconography of mystics and martyr saints, the illustrations establish a parallel between her and a Venus. Thus, the illustrations add an erotic and joyful dimension to the story in addition to the representation of the woman. According to Mary Meigs' interpretation, a woman can play an active and positive role in this fictional world.

Consequently, it is important to underline that Blais' novel and Meigs' illustrations construct Héloïse's character in very different ways. In the novel, references to masturbation and sexual activity are sometimes ironic, sometimes veiled. In contrast, the drawings show Héloïse naked and touching herself. The difference comes from an eroticized representation of the female body and from jubilant nudity and sexuality in the illustrations. It is clear that these traits simplify the character's sexuality since she is no longer religious or masochistic.

FROM TEXT TO IMAGE: REGENERATION

Meigs' drawings are thus more a reconstruction than a representation of Blais' novel. Her illustrations aim to capture the human and emotional essence of the fictional characters. The drawings often surpass the function as illustration to become candid portraits of humanity as well as a critique of accepted truths. Moreover, the similarities and differences between the text and the image serve to illuminate the meaning and organization of the illustrated edition. Blais' literary portraits inspire Meigs, but the artist effects transformations and significant recreations. The illustration has the power to act on the reader and to transform the written word, even to compromise the text's status as the unique source of information on the story, its themes and its characters.

The role of the illustrator is frequently to "materialise, express her vision and her personal thoughts, at the risk of producing conflicting meanings."[11] However, rather than speak of discrepancies or even of betrayal in the transfer from literary portrait to visual portrait, it is more relevant to speak of renewal. Mary Meigs' drawings renew not only the meaning attributed to the character of

_____

[11] Gérard Gréverand, *op. cit.*, 83.

Héloïse, but also the interpretation of the novel itself. Marie-Claire Blais' "dancing, waltzing writing," one that plays on "all forms of reversal,"[12] as Gilles Marcotte aptly puts it, is made more complex because the illustrations make it both more macabre and more comic. The principle of regeneration functions in the text, and in the illustrations, as well as in the reciprocal influence of one on the other. If art and literature have as their objectives the creation and the renewal of ideas, if they constitute spaces of understanding and contemplation, the illustrated novel does so doubly. Each medium examines the imaginary world of the other, contesting it, validating it, representing it, and above all reconstructing it.

Mount Allison University

---

[12] Gilles Marcotte. *Le Roman à l'imparfait. La "Révolution tranquille" du roman québécois.* Montréal: L'Hexagone, 1989 [2nd Edition], p. 181.

Bibliography

Blais, Marie-Claire. *Une Saison dans la vie d'Emmanuel*, illustrated by Mary Meigs. Montréal: Éditions du Jour, 1968.

Bourque, Dominique. "Héloïse ou la voix du silence dans *Une Saison dans la vie d'Emmanuel*." *Voix et Images* 23, 68 (1998): 329-345.

Greffard, Madeleine. "*Une Saison dans la vie d'Emmanuel*, kaléidoscope de la réalité québécoise." *Les Cahiers de Sainte-Marie* 1 (1966): 19-24.

Gréverand, Gérard. "L'Illustration des *Fables* de la Fontaine, 1668-1980." *Iconographie et littérature. D'un art à l'autre*. Ed. Alain Niderst. Paris: Presses universitaires de France, 1983: 81-96.

Lacasse, Roger. "Un Livre de grand luxe relié et imprimé à Québec lancé sous peu." *L'Action Québec* (16 December 1968): 7.

Marcotte, Gilles. *Le Roman à l'imparfait. La "Révolution tranquille" du roman québécois*. Montréal: L'Hexagone [2ᵉ édition], 1989.

Meigs, Mary. *Lily Briscoe: A Self-Portrait*. Vancouver: Talonbooks, 1981.

Meigs, Mary. "From Lily Briscoe, A Self-Portrait, with Five Drawings for a Novel By Marie-Claire Blais – *Les Nuits de l'Underground*." *Exile Quarterly* 6, Nº 1/2 (1979): 39-64.

Meigs, Mary. *Illustrations for Two Novels by Marie-Claire Blais: The Manuscripts of Pauline Archange and St. Lawrence Blues*. Toronto: Exile Editions, 1977.

Meigs, Mary. "Four Drawings" [for *St. Lawrence Blues* by Marie-Claire Blais]. *Exile Quarterly* 1, Nº 4 (1974): 106-109.

Mitterand, Henri. "Coup de pistolet dans un concert: *Une Saison dans la vie d'Emmanuel*." *Voix et Images* 2, 3 (1977): 407-417.

Robert, Guy. "Une Saison violente." *Vie des arts* 58 (1970): 109-110.

Questions for Discussion and Essays

1. Emmanuel, the title character, is not the main character of *A Season in the Life of Emmanuel*. Or is he? How were your expectations as a reader informed by the title and how did those expectations change over the course of your reading? Discuss the character of Emmanuel and his importance to the novel.

2. The mother and father figures are virtually absent throughout the novel. Discuss the representations of parenthood and the social conditions affecting their actions and choices as parents. What are the qualities that Grand-mère possesses that make her "immortal"? How does she affect the lives of her grandchildren over the course of the book?

3. The Catholic Church is, arguably, omnipresent in the novel. Discuss how traditional Catholic values are expressed and problematized by the actions of the characters in the book. What aspects of Catholic doctrine or practice do you think Blais interrogates through her narration?

4. The imaginative lives of the characters protect them but also leave them open to vulnerabilities from the outside world. How are these imaginative lives expressed in the book? What kind of language does Blais use to best convey these interior fears and desires? How do the characters' imaginative and spiritual lives differ from their everyday realities? How does Blais convey these differences?

5. Emmanuel is the sixteenth child in the family. How many of the other children can you name? What characteristics do you

remember about them? How do the siblings feel about each other? What different kinds of relationships do they have with each other and how are these expressed or explored in the novel?

6. What does Blais accomplish with her unconventional prose style? Does she cause you to think or react to these characters and their lives in new or interesting ways? What sort of atmosphere does she create and how would you describe its aesthetics?

7. Are there implied social critiques in the novel? If so, how are the social issues explored and what arguments do you think Blais might be making for change?

8. What events of the novel are represented by the selected Mary Meigs drawings? How do they enlighten or inform your reading of the book? Do her representations remain faithful to the aims or effects of the book? If so, how?

9. Rebelliousness and stubbornness emerge as sister-traits possessed by some of the most compelling characters in the novel, particularly Grand-mère Antoinette, Jean-Le Maigre, Number Seven, Héloïse, and Emmanuel. Discuss how rebelliousness and stubbornness inform their decisions and their destinies.

10. How is *A Season in the Life of Emmanuel* relevant today? Can you draw parallels between the social circumstances the characters live in and the lives of others today in the twenty-first century? How far are you able to empathize with the characters' plights? Are the fears and desires of the characters represented in the novel very different from your own? If so, what important insights into human nature do you take away with you from this reading experience?

Selected Works by Marie-Claire Blais

Coltman, Derek (trans). *The Manuscripts of Pauline Archange.*
Toronto: McClelland and Stewart, 1982. [Originally published
in French in 1968.]

Coltman, Derek (trans). *A Season in the Life of Emmanuel*
Toronto: Exile Editions Classics Series, 2008. [Originally published in French in 1965].

Dunlop, Carol (trans). *Deaf to the City.*
Toronto: Exile Editions Classics Series, 2006. [Originally published in French in 1979].

Ellenwood, Ray (trans). *Nights in the Underground.*
Toronto: Exile Editions Classics Series, 2006. [Originally published in French in 1978.]

Fischman, Sheila (trans). *The Wolf.*
Toronto: Exile Editions Classics Series, 2008. [Originally published in French in 1970.]

Gaboriau, Linda (trans). *American Notebooks: A Writer's Journey.*
Burnaby, BC: Talonbooks, 1996. [Originally published in French
in 1993.]

Lawrence, Merloyd (trans). *Mad Shadows.*
Toronto: McClelland and Stewart, 1990. [Originally published
in French in 1959.]

Spencer, Nigel (trans). *Augustino and the Choir of Destruction.*
Toronto: House of Anansi, 2007. [Originally published in French
in 2005.]

Selected Books and Articles on Marie-Claire Blais and *A Season in the Life of Emmanuel*

Anderson, Margaret. "The Church in Marie-Claire Blais' *A Season in the Life of Emmanuel.*"
Sphinx: A Magazine of Literature and Society 7 (1977): 40-46.

Bell, Kirsty. "Portraits of Héloïse in the Illustrated Edition of *A Season in the Life of Emmanuel.*"
[Reprinted in this book. Originally published in Janine Ricouart and Roseanna Du-fault's book *Visions poétiques de Marie-Claire Blais*. Montréal: Les éditions du remue-ménage, 2008.]

Callaghan, Barry. "An Interview with Marie-Claire Blais."
Tamarack Review 37 (1965): 29-34.

Gordon, Jan B. "An 'Incandescence of Suffering': The Fiction of Marie-Claire Blais."
Modern Fiction Studies. 22 (1976): 467-84.

Green, Mary Jean. *Marie-Claire Blais.*
New York: Twayne Publishers, 1995.

Green, Mary Jean. "Redefining the Maternal: Women's Relationships in the Fiction of Marie-Claire Blais." Paula Gilbert Lewis et al. *Traditionalism, Nationalism, and Feminism: Women Writers of Quebec.* Paula Gilbert Lewis (editor).
Westport, CT: Greenwood, 1985: 125-39.

Laurent, Françoise. *L'Oeuvre Romanesque de Marie-Claire Blais.*
Montréal: Editions Fides Inc. Collection Approches, 1986.

Lecker, Robert A. "The Aesthetics of Deception: Marie-Claire
Blais' *A Season in the Life of Emmanuel.*"
Essays on Canadian Writing 22 (1976): 467-84.

Oore, Irène. *Marie-Claire Blais: An Annotated Bibliography.*
Toronto: ECW Press, 1998.

Ricouart Janine et Roseanna Dufault. *Visions poétiques de Marie-
Claire Blais.*
Montréal: Les editions du remue-ménage, 2008.

Stratford, Philip. *Marie-Claire Blais.*
Toronto: Forum House, 1971.

Related Reading

Aquin, Hubert. *Next Episode.* Sheila Fischman (trans).
Toronto: McClelland and Stewart, 2001. [Originally published in French in 1965.]

Aquin, Hubert. *Writing Quebec: Selected Essays.* Paul Gibson (trans). Edmonton: University of Alberta Press, 1988.

Bessette, Gérard. *Not for Every Eye: A Novel.* Glen Shortliffe (trans). Toronto: Exile Editions, 1999. [Original published in French in 1960.]

Hébert, Anne. *Kamouraska.* Norman Shapiro (trans).
Toronto: House of Anansi, 2002. [Originally published in French in 1973.]

Hémon, Louis. *Maria Chapdelaine.* W.H. Blake (trans).
Don Mills: Stoddard, 1992. [Originally published in French in 1916.]

Meigs, Mary. *Illustrations for Two Novels by Marie-Claire Blais: The Manuscripts of Pauline Archange* and *St. Lawrence Blues.* Toronto: Exile Editions, 1977.

Ringuet. *Thirty Acres.* Fexil and Dorothea Walter (trans).
Toronto: McClelland and Steward, 1989. [Originally published in French in 1938.]

Roy, Gabrielle. *The Tin Flute*. Alan Brown (trans.)
Toronto: McClelland and Stewart, 1989. [Originally published in French in 1945.]

Stratford, Philip. *All the Polarities: Comparative Studies in Contemporary Canadian Novels in English and French.*
Toronto: ECW Press, 1986.

Teleky, Richard (editor). *The Oxford Book of French-Canadian
Short Stories.* Marie-Claire Blais (introduction).
Toronto: Oxford University Press, 1983.

Websites of Interest

http://www.thecanadianencyclopedia.com/index.cfm?PgNm=TC
E&Params=A1ARTA0000810

http://www.collectionscanada.gc.ca/writers/027005-1000-e.html

http://www.athabascau.ca/writers/mcblais.html

http://www.britannica.com/eb/article-9015578/Marie-Claire-
Blais

http://www.movingimages.ca/catalogue/Art/marieclaireblais.html

This book is entirely printed on FSC certified paper.

Mixed Sources
Product group from well-managed
forests and recycled wood or fiber
www.fsc.org Cert no. SGS-COC-2624
© 1996 Forest Stewardship Council